Marion

BY
VICTOR HUGO

MARION DE LORME

DRAMATIS PERSONÆ

MARION DE LORME.

DIDIER.

LOUIS XIII.

MARQUIS DE SAVERNY.

MARQUIS DE NANGIS.

L'ANGELY.

M. DE LAFFEMAS.

DUKE DE BELLEGARDE.

MARQUIS DE BRICHANTEAU,

COUNT DE GASSÉ,

VISCOUNT DE BOUCHAVANNES,

CHEVALIER DE ROCHEBARON,

COUNT DE VILLAC,

CHEVALIER DE MONTPESAT,

Officers of the Regiment of Anjou.

DUKE DE BEAUPRÉAU.

VISCOUNT DE ROHAN.

ABBÉ DE GONDI.

COUNT DE CHARNACÉ.

SCARAMOUCHE,

GRACIEUX,   *Provincial comedians.*

TAILLEBRAS,

COUNCILOR OF THE GREAT CHAMBER.

TOWN CRIER.	CAPTAIN.
A JAILER.	A REGISTRAR.
THE EXECUTIONER.	FIRST WORKMAN.
SECOND WORKMAN.	THIRD WORKMAN.
A LACKEY.	DAME ROSE.

Provincial Comedians, Guards, Populace, Nobles, Pages.
1638.

MARION DE LORME
ACT I
THE MEETING

SCENE.—*Blois. A bed-chamber. A window opening on a balcony at the back. To the right, a table with a lamp, and an armchair. To the left a door, covered by a portière of tapestry. In the background a bed*
SCENE I
MARION DE LORME, *in a very elegant wrapper, sitting beside the table, embroidering.* MARQUIS DE SAVERNY, *very young man, blonde, without mustache, dressed in the latest fashion of 1638*

SAVERNY (*approaching* MARION *and trying to embrace her*).

Let us be reconciled, my sweet Marie!

MARION (*pushing him away*).

Not such close reconciliation, please!
SAVERNY (*insisting*).
Just one kiss!
MARION (*angrily*).
Marquis!
SAVERNY.
What a rage! Your mouthHad sweeter manners, not so long ago!
MARION.
Ah, you forget!
SAVERNY.
No, I remember, dear.
MARION (*aside*).
The bore! the tiresome creature!
SAVERNY.
Speak, fair one!What does this swift, unkind departure mean?While all are seeking you at Place Royale,Why do you hide yourself at Blois? Traitress,What have you done here all these two long months?
MARION.
I do what pleases me, and what I wishIs right. I'm free, my lord!
SAVERNY.
Free! Yes. But thoseWhose hearts you've stolen, are they also free?I? Gondi, who omitted half his MassThe other day, because he had a duelUpon his hands for you? Nesmond, D'Arquien,The two Caussades, Pressigny, whom your flightHas left so wretched, so morose, evenTheir wives wish you were back in Paris, thatThey might have gayer husbands!
MARION (*smiling*).
Beauvillain?
SAVERNY.
Is still in love.
MARION.
Cereste?
SAVERNY.
Adores you yet.
MARION.
And Pons?
SAVERNY.
Oh, as for him, he hates you!
MARION.
ProofHe is the only one who loves me! Well,The President?[*Laughing.*] The old man! What's his name?
[*Laughing more heartily.*
Leloup!
SAVERNY.
He's waiting for you, and meanwhileHe keeps your portrait and sings odes to it.
MARION.
He's loved me two years now, in effigy.
SAVERNY.
He'd much prefer to burn you. Tell me howYou keep away from such dear friends.
MARION (*serious, and lowering her eyes*).
That's justThe reason, Marquis; to be frank with you,Those brilliant follies which seduced my youthHave given me much more misery than joy.In a retreat, a convent cell, perhaps,I want to try to expiate my life.
SAVERNY.
I'll wager there's a love-tale behind that.
MARION.
You dare to think—

2

SAVERNY.
That never a nun's veilSurmounted eyes so full of earthly fire.It could not be. You love some poor provincial!For shame! To end a fine romance with suchA page!

MARION.
It isn't true!

SAVERNY.
Let's make a wager!

MARION.
Dame Rose, what time is it?

DAME ROSE (*outside*).
Almost midnight!

MARION (*aside*).
Midnight!

SAVERNY.
That is a most ingenious wayOf saying, "Time to go."

MARION.
I live retired,Receiving no one, and unknown to all.Besides, 'tis dangerous to be out late:The street is lonely, full of robbers.

SAVERNY.
Well,They can rob me.

MARION.
And oftentimes they kill!

SAVERNY.
Good! they can kill me.

MARION.
But—

SAVERNY.
You are divine!But I'll not stir one foot before I knowWho this gay shepherd is, who's routed us!

MARION.
There's no one!

SAVERNY.
I will be discreet. We courtiers,Whom people think so mad, so curiousAnd spiteful, are maligned. We gossip, butWe never talk! You're silent?[*Sits down.*] Then I'll stay!

MARION.
What does it matter? Well, it's true! I love!I'm waiting for him!

SAVERNY.
That's the way to talk!That's right! Where is it you expect him?

MARION.
Here!

SAVERNY.
When?

MARION.
Now! [*She goes to the balcony and listens.*Hark! that is he perhaps.[*Coming back.*] 'Tis not.Now are you satisfied?

SAVERNY.
Not quite!

MARION.
Please go!

SAVERNY.
I want to know his name, this proud gallant,For whose reception I am thus dismissed.

MARION.
Didier is all the name I know for him.Marie is all the name he knows for me.

SAVERNY (*laughing*).
Is't true?

MARION.

3

Yes, true!

SAVERNY.

This is a pastoral,And no mistake. 'Tis Racan, pure! To enter,I have no doubt he scales the wall.

MARION.

Perhaps.Please go! [*Aside.*] He wearies me to death!

SAVERNY (*becoming serious*).

Of courseHe's noble.

MARION.

I don't know.

SAVERNY.

What?

[*To* MARION, *who is gently pushing him toward the door.*
I am going! [*Coming back.*Just one word more! I had forgotten. Look!

[*He draws a book out of his pocket and gives it to* MARION.
An author who is not a fool, did this.It's making a great stir.

MARION (*reading the title*).

"Love's Garland"—ah!"To Marion de Lorme."

SAVERNY.

They talk of nothingBut this in Paris. That book and "The Cid"Are the successful efforts of the day.

MARION (*taking the book*).

It's very civil of you; now, good-night!

SAVERNY.

What is the use of fame? Alack-a-day!To come to Blois and love a rustic! Bah!

MARION (*calling to* DAME ROSE).

Take care of the Marquis, and show him out!

SAVERNY (*saluting her*).

Ah, Marion, you've degenerated! [*He goes out.*

SCENE II

MARION, *afterward* DIDIER

MARION (*alone, shuts the door by which* SAVERNY *went out*).

Go—Go quickly! Oh, I feared lest Didier—

[*Midnight strikes.*
Hark!It's striking midnight! Didier should be here!

[*She goes to the balcony and looks into the street.*
No one!

[*She comes back and sits down impatiently.*
Late! To be late—so soon!

[*A young man appears behind the balustrade of the balcony, jumps over it lightly, enters, places his cloak and sword on the armchair. Costume of the day: all black: boots. He takes one step forward, pauses and contemplates* MARION, *sitting with her eyes cast down.*
At last!

[*Reproachfully.*
To let me count the hour alone!

DIDIER (*seriously*).

I fearedTo enter!

MARION (*hurt*).

Ah!

DIDIER (*without noticing it*).

Down there, outside the wall,I was o'ercome with pity. Pity? yes,For you! I, poor, accursed, unfortunate,Stood there a long time thinking, ere I came!"Up there an angel waits," I thought, "in virgin grace,Untouched by sin—a being chaste and fair,To whose sweet face shining on life's pathwayEach passer-by should bend his knees and pray.I, who am but a vagrant 'mongst the crowd,Why should I seek to stir that placid stream?Why should I pluck that lily? With the breathOf human passion, why should I consentTo cloud the azure of that

4

radiant soul?Since in her loyalty she trusts to me,Since virtue shields her with its sanctity,Have I a right to take her gift of love,To bring my storms into her perfect day?"

MARION (*aside*).

This is theology, it seems to me!I wonder if he is a Huguenot?

DIDIER.

But when your tender voice fell on my ear,I wrestled with my doubts no more—I came.

MARION.

Oh, then you heard me speaking—that is strange!

DIDIER.

Yes; with another person.

MARION (*quickly*).

With Dame Rose!She talks just like a man, don't you think so?Such a strong voice! Ah, well, since you are hereI am no longer angry! Come, sit down.

[*Indicating a place at her side.*

Sit here!

DIDIER.

No! at your feet.

[*He sits on a stool at* MARION'S *feet and looks at her for some moments in complete silence.*

Hear me, Marie!I have no name but Didier—never knewMy father nor my mother. I was left,A baby, on the threshold of a church.A woman, old, belonging to the people,Preserved me, was my mother and my nurse.She brought me up a Christian, then she diedAnd left me all she had—nine hundred francsA year, on which I live. To be aloneAt twenty is a sad and bitter thing!I traveled—saw mankind: I learned to hateA few and to despise the rest. For onThis tarnished mirror we call human life,I saw nothing but pride and miseryAnd pain; so that, although I'm young, I'm old,And am as weary of the world as areThe men who leave it. Never touched a thingThat did not tear and lacerate my soul!Although the world was bad, I found men worse.Thus I have lived; alone and poor and sad,Until you came, and you have set things right.I hardly know you. At the corner ofA Paris street you first appeared to me.Then afterward I met you, and I thoughtYour eyes were sweet, your speech was beautiful!I was afraid of loving you, and fled!But destiny is strange: I found you here,I find you everywhere, as if you wereMy guardian angel. So at last, my loveGrew powerful, resistless, and I feltI must talk with you. You were willing. NowThey're at your service, both my heart and life.I will do anything that you wish done.If there is any man or anythingThat troubles you, or you have any whimAnd somebody must die to satisfy it—Must die, and make no sign—and feel 'twas worthDeath any time to see you smile; if youNeed such a man, speak, lady: I am here!

MARION (*smiling*).

You've a strange nature, but I love you so!

DIDIER.

You love me! Ah, take care! One dare not saySuch words in any careless way! Love me?Oh, do you know what loving means? What 'tisTo feel love take possession of our blood,Become our daily breath? To feel this thingWhich long has smoldered burst to flame, and riseA great, majestic, purifying fire?To feel it burn up clean within our heartsThe refuse other passions have left there?This love, hopeless indeed, but limitless,Which outlives all things, even happiness—Is this the kind of love you mean?

MARION (*touched*).

Indeed!

DIDIER.

You do not know it, but I love you so!From that first time I saw you, my dark lifeWas shot with sunlight streaming from your eyes;Since then all's different. To me you seemSome wonderful creation, not of earth.My life, in whose dark gloom I groaned so long,Grows almost beautiful when you are by.For 'til you came, I'd wandered, suffered, wept;I'd struggled, fallen—but I had not loved.

MARION.

Poor Didier!

5

DIDIER.

Speak, Marie!

MARION.

Well, then, I do.I love with just this love—love you as muchAnd maybe more than you love me! It wasNot destiny that brought me here. 'Twas IWho came, who followed you, and I am yours!

DIDIER (*falling on his knees*).

Oh, do not cheat me! Give me truth, Marie!If to my ardent love your love responds,The world holds no possession rich as mine!My whole life, kneeling at your feet, will beOne sigh of speechless, blinding ecstasy.But do not cheat me!

MARION.

Do you want a proofOf love, my Didier?

DIDIER.

Yes!

MARION.

Then speak!

DIDIER.

You are—Quite free?

MARION (*embarrassed*).

Free? Yes!

DIDIER.

Then take me for a brother,For a protector—be my wife?

MARION (*aside*).

His wife!Ah, why am I not worthy?

DIDIER.

You consent?

MARION.

I—can—

DIDIER.

Don't say it, please—I understand!An orphan, without fortune! What a fool!Give back my pain, my gloom, my solitude!Farewell!

[*He starts to go;* MARION *holds him back.*

MARION.

Didier, what are you saying?

[*She bursts into tears.*

DIDIER.

True!But why this hesitation? [*Going back to her.*Can't you feel!The ecstasy of being, each to each, a world,A country, heaven; in some deserted spotTo hide a happiness kings could not buy.

MARION.

It would be heaven!

DIDIER.

Will you have it? Come!

MARION.

[*Aside.*] Accursed woman! [*Aloud.*] No, it cannot be.

[*She tears herself from out his arms, and falls on the armchair.*

DIDIER (*freezingly*).

The offer was not generous, I know.You've answered me. I'll speak of it no more!Good-by!

MARION. (*aside*).

Alack, the day I pleased him! [*Aloud.*] Stay!I'll tell you. You have hurt me to the soul.I will explain—

DIDIER (*coldly*).

What were you reading, madame,When I came?

[*Takes the book from the table and reads.*

"To Marion de Lorme.Love's Garland!" Yes, the beauty of the day!

6

[*Throwing the book violently to the floor.*
Vile creature! a dishonor to her sex!
MARION. (*trembling*).
But—she—
DIDIER.
What are you doing with such books?How came they here?
MARION. (*inaudibly, and looking down*).
They came by chance.
DIDIER.
Do you—You who have eyes so pure, a brow so chaste—Do you know what she is—this woman? Well,She's beautiful in body, and deformedIn soul! A Phryne, selling everywhere,To every man, her love, which is an insult,An infamy!
MARION (*her head in her hands*).
My God!
[*A noise of footsteps, a clashing of swords outside, and cries.*
VOICE IN THE STREET.
Help! Murder! Help!
DIDIER (*surprised*).
What noise is that out there upon the square?
[*Cries continue.*
VOICE IN THE STREET.
Help! Murder! Help!
DIDIER (*looking from the balcony*).
They're killing some one! Ha!
[*He takes his sword and step's over the balustrade.* MARION *rises, runs to him and tries to hold him back by his cloak.*
MARION.
Don't, Didier, if you love me! They'll kill you!Don't go!
DIDIER (*jumping down into the street*).
He is the one they're going to kill!Poor man! [*Outside, to combatants.*Stand off! Hold firmly, sir, and push!
[*Clashing of swords.*
There, wretch!
[*Noise of swords, voices, and footsteps.*
MARION. (*on the balcony, terrified*).
Just Heaven! They are six 'gainst two!
VOICE IN THE STREET.
This man—he is the devil!
[*The clashing of swords subsides little by little, then entirely ceases. The sounds of footsteps become indistinct.* DIDIER *reappears scaling the balcony.*
DIDIER (*outside of the balcony and turned toward the street*).
You are safe;Now go your way!
SAVERNY (*from outside*).
Not 'til I've grasped your hand—Not 'til I've thanked you, if you please!
DIDIER.
Pass on!I will consider myself thanked.
SAVERNY.
Not so!I mean to thank you. [*Scaling balcony.*
DIDIER.
Can't you speak from thereAnd say "I thank you" without coming up?
SCENE III
MARION, DIDIER, SAVERNY
SAVERNY (*jumping into the room, sword in hand*).
Upon my soul! 'Tis a strange chivalryTo save my life and push me from the door!The door—that is to say, the window! No,They shall not say one of my familyWas bravely rescued by a noblemanAnd did not in return say "Marquis—" Pray,What is your name?

7

DIDIER.
Didier.
SAVERNY.
Didier—of what?
DIDIER.
Didier, of nothing! People kill you, andI help you—that is all! Now go!
SAVERNY.
Indeed!That's your way, is it? Why not have letThose traitors kill me? 'Twould have pleased me more.For without you I'd be a dead man now.Six thieves against me! Dead! Of course! What else?Six daggers against one thin sword—
[*Perceiving* MARION, *who has been trying to avoid him.*
Oh, ho!You're not alone! At last I understand!I'm robbing you of pleasure. Pardon me![*Aside.*] I'd like to see the lady!
[*Approaches* MARION, *who is trembling: he recognizes her.*
It is you!
[*Indicating* DIDIER.
Then he's the one!
MARION (*low*).
Hush! You will ruin all!
SAVERNY (*bowing*).
Madame!
MARION (*low*).
I love for the first time!
DIDIER (*aside*).
'Sdeath!That man is looking at her with bold eyes.
[*He overturns the lamp with a blow.*
SAVERNY.
You put the lamp out, sir?
DIDIER.
It would be wiseFor us to leave together, and at once.
SAVERNY.
So be it, then! I follow you!
[*To* MARION, *whom he salutes profoundly.*
Madame,Farewell!
DIDIER (*aside*).
What a rare coxcomb![*Aloud to* SAVERNY.] Come, sir, come!
SAVERNY.
You're brusk, but I'm in debt to you for life.If ever you should need fraternal friendship,Count upon me, Marquis de Saverny,Paris, Hôtel de Nesle.
DIDIER.
Enough, sir! Come![*Aside.*] To see her thus examined by a fool!
[*They go out by the balcony. The voice of* DIDIER *is heard outside.*
Your road lies that way. Mine lies here!
SCENE IV
MARION, DAME ROSE
MARION (*remains absorbed a moment, then calls*).
Dame Rose!
[DAME ROSE *appears.* MARION *points to the window.*
Go shut it!
[DAME ROSE, *having shut the window, turns and sees* MARION *wiping away a tear.*
DAME ROSE (*aside*).
She is weeping![*Aloud.*] It is timeTo sleep, madame!
MARION.
Yes, time for you—you people.
[*Undoing her hair.*
Come, help me to undress!

8

DAME ROSE (*helping her to undress*).
The gentlemanTo-night was pleasant. Is he rich?
MARION.
Not rich.
DAME ROSE.
But gallant.
MARION.
No, nor gallant.
[*Turning to* DAME ROSE.
He did notSo much as kiss my hand!
DAME ROSE.
What use is he?
MARION (*pensive*).
I love him!

ACT II
THE ENCOUNTER
SCENE.—*Blois. The door of a public-house. A square. In the background the city of Blois is visible in the form of an amphitheater, also the towers of St. Nicholas upon the hill, which is covered with houses*
SCENE I
COUNT DE GASSÉ, MARQUIS DE BRICHANTEAU, VISCOUNT DE BOUCHAVANNES, CHEVALIER DE ROCHEBARON. *They are seated at tables in front of the door: some are smoking, the others are throwing dice and drinking. Afterward*CHEVALIER DE MONTPESAT, COUNT DE VILLAC; *afterward* L'ANGELY; *afterward* THE TOWN-CRIER *and The Populace*
BRICHANTEAU (*rising, to* GASSÉ, *who enters*).
Gassé! [*They shake hands.*You are come to joinThe regiment at Blois: our complimentsUpon your burial. [*Examining his clothes.*Ah!
GASSÉ.
It is the style—This orange with blue ribbons.
[*Folding his arms and curling his mustache.*
You must knowThat Blois is forty miles from Paris!
BRICHANTEAU.
Yes,It's China!
GASSÉ.
That makes womankind rebel:To follow us they must exile themselves.
BOUCHAVANNES (*turning from the game*).
You come from Paris?
ROCHEBARON (*taking out his pipe*).
Is there any news?
GASSÉ (*bowing*).
No, nothing. Corneille still upsets all heads.Guiche has obtained the order; Ast is duke.Of trifles, plenty—thirty HuguenotsWere hung; a quantity of duels. OnThe third, D'Angennes fought Arquien on accountOf wearing point of Genoa; the tenth,Lavardie had a rendezvous with Pons,Because he'd taken Sourdis' wife from him.Sourdis and D'Ailly met about a creatureIn the theater Mondori. On the ninth,Lachâtre fought with Nogent because he wroteThree rhymes of Colletet's badly; MargaillanWith Gorde, about the time of day; D'HumièreWith Gondi on the way to walk in church;And all the Brissacs 'gainst all the SoubisesFor some bet on a horse against a dog.Then Caussade and Latournelle fought for nothing—Merely for fun: Caussade killed Latournelle.
BRICHANTEAU.
Gay Paris! Duels have begun again.
GASSÉ.
It is the fashion!
BRICHANTEAU.
Feasts and love and fighting!There is the only place to live![*Yawning.*] All oneCan do here is to die of weariness.[*To* GASSÉ.] You say Caussade killed Latournelle?

9

GASSÉ.

He did,With a good gash!

[*Examining* ROCHEBARON'S *sleeves.*

What's that you wear, my friend?Those trimmings are not fashionable now.What!
cords and buttons? Nothing could be worse.You must have bows and ribbons.

BRICHANTEAU.

Pray repeatThe list of duels. How about the King?What does he say?

GASSÉ.

The Cardinal's enragedAnd means to stop it.

BOUCHAVANNES.

Any news from camp?

GASSÉ.

I think we captured Figuère by surprise—Or else we lost it.[*Reflecting.*] Yes, that's it.
'Tis lost!They took it from us.

ROCHEBARON.

Ah! What said the King?

GASSÉ.

The Cardinal is most dissatisfied.

BRICHANTEAU.

How is the Court? I hope the King is well.

GASSÉ.

Alas! the Cardinal has fever andThe gout, and goes out only in a litter.

BRICHANTEAU.

Queer! We talk King, you answer Cardinal!

GASSÉ.

It is the fashion!

BOUCHAVANNES.

So there's nothing new!

GASSÉ.

Did I say so? There's been a miracle,A prodigy, which has amazed all ParisFor two
months past; the flight, the disappearance—

BRICHANTEAU.

Go on! Of whom?

GASSÉ.

Of Marion de Lorme,The fairest of the fair!

BRICHANTEAU (*with an air of mystery*).

Here's news for you.She's here!

GASSÉ.

At Blois?

BRICHANTEAU.

Incognito!

GASSÉ.

What! she?In this place? Oh, you must be jesting, sir!Fair Marion, who sets the
fashions! Bah!This Blois is the antipodes of Paris.Observe! How ugly, old, ungainly, 'tis!Even
those towers—

[*Indicating the towers of St. Nicholas.*

Uncouth and countrified!

ROCHEBARON.

That's true.

BRICHANTEAU.

Won't you believe Saverny whenHe says he saw her, hidden somewhere withA lover,
and this lover saved his lifeWhen thieves attacked him in the street at night?—Good thieves,
who took his purse for charity,And just desired his watch to know the time.

GASSÉ.

You tell me wonders!

ROCHEBARON (*to* BRICHANTEAU).

Are you sure of it?
BRICHANTEAU.
As sure as that I have six silver bezantsUpon a field of azure. SavernyHas no desire, at present, but to findThis man.
BOUCHAVANNES.
He ought to find him at her house.
BRICHANTEAU.
She's changed her name and lodging, and all traceOf her is lost.
[MARION *and* DIDIER *cross the back of the stage slowly without being noticed by the talkers; they enter a small door in one of the houses on the side.*
GASSÉ.
To have to come to BloisTo find our Marion, a provincial!
[*Enter* COUNT DE VILLAC *and* CHEVALIER DE MONTPESAT, *disputing loudly.*
VILLAC.
No!I tell you no!
MONTPESAT.
And I—I tell you, yes!
VILLAC.
Corneille is bad!
MONTPESAT.
To treat Corneille like that—The author of "The Cid" and of "Melite."
VILLAC.
"Melite"? Well, I will grant you that is good;But he degenerated after that,As they all do. I'll do the best I canTo satisfy you: talk about "Melite,""The Gallery of the Palace," but "The Cid!"What is it, pray?
GASSÉ (*to* MONTPESAT).
You are conservative.
MONTPESAT.
"The Cid" is good!
VILLAC.
I tell you it is bad!Your "Cid"—why Scudéry can crush it withA touch! Look at the style! It deals with thingsExtraordinary; has a vulgar tone;Describes things plainly by their common names;Besides, it is obscene, against the law!"The Cid" has not the right to wed Chimène!Now have you read Pyramus, Bradamante?When Corneille writes such tragedies, I'll read!
ROCHEBARON (*to* MONTPESAT).
"The Great and Last Soliman" of Mairet,You must read that: that is fine tragedy!But for your "Cid."
VILLAC.
What self-conceit he has!Does he not think he equals Boisrobert,Mairet, Gombault, Serisay, Chapelain,Bautru, Desmarets, Malleville, Faret,Cherisy, Gomberville, Colletet, Giry,Duryer—indeed, all the Academy?
BRICHANTEAU (*laughing compassionately and shrugging his shoulders*).
Good!
VILLAC.
Then the gentleman deigns to create!Create! Faith! after Garnier, Theophile,And Hardy! Oh, the coxcomb! To create!An easy thing! As if the famous mindsHad left behind them any unused thing.On that point Chapelain rebukes him well!
ROCHEBARON.
Corneille's a peasant!
BOUCHAVANNES.
Yet, Monsieur Godeau,Bishop of Grasse, says he's a man of wit.
MONTPESAT.
Much wit!
VILLAC.
If he would write some other way—Would follow Aristotle and good style.

11

GASSÉ.

Come, gentlemen, make peace. One thing is sure,Corneille is now the fashion: takes the placeOf Garnier, just as in our day felt hatsHave replaced velvet *mortiers*.

MONTPESAT.

For CorneilleI am, and for felt hats!

GASSÉ (*to* MONTPESAT).

You are too rash![*To* VILLAC.] Garnier is very fine. I'm neutral; butCorneille has also his good points.

VILLAC.

Agreed!

ROCHEBARON.

Agreed! He is a witty fellow andI like him!

BRICHANTEAU.

He has no nobility!

ROCHEBARON.

A name so commonplace offends the ear.

BOUCHAVANNES.

A family of petty lawyers, whoHave gnawed at ducats 'til they obtained sous.

[L'ANGELY *enters, seats himself at a table alone, and in silence. He is dressed in black velvet with gold trimming.*

VILLAC.

Well, if the public like his rhapsodiesThe day of tragic-comedy is past.I swear to you the theater is doomed.It is because this Richelieu—

GASSÉ (*looking across at* L'ANGELY).

Say, *lordship*,Or else speak lower.

BRICHANTEAU.

Hell take this eminence!Is't not enough to manage everything?To rule our soldiers, finances, and us,Without controlling our poor language too?

BOUCHAVANNES.

Down with this Richelieu, who flatters, kills:Man of the red hand and the scarlet robe!

ROCHEBARON.

Of what use is the King?

BRICHANTEAU.

In darkness, we—That is the people—march: eyes on a torch.He is the torch: the King's the lantern whichIn its bright glass protects the flame from wind.

BOUCHAVANNES.

Oh, could our swords blow such a wind some dayAs to extinguish this devouring fire!

ROCHEBARON.

If every one had the same mind as I!

BRICHANTEAU.

We would unite—[*To* BOUCHAVANNES.] What do you think, Viscount?

BOUCHAVANNES.

We'd give him one perfidious, useful blow!

L'ANGELY (*rising, with gloomy tone*).

Conspiring! Young men! Think of Marillac!

[*All shudder: turn away, and are silent with terror; all fix their eyes on* L'ANGELY, *who silently resumes his seat.*

VILLAC (*taking* MONTPESAT *aside*).

My lord, when we were talking of Corneille,You spoke in tones that irritated me.In my turn I would like to say two wordsTo you—

MONTPESAT.

With sword—

VILLAC.

Yes.

MONTPESAT.

Or with pistol?

12

VILLAC.
Both!
MONTPESAT (*taking his arm*).
Let's go and find some corner in the town.
L'ANGELY (*rising*).
A duel, sirs? Remember Boutteville.
[*New consternation among the young men.* VILLAC *and* MONTPESAT *separate, keeping their eyes fixed on* L'ANGELY.
ROCHEBARON.
Who is this man in black who frightens us?
L'ANGELY.
I'm L'Angely. I'm jester to the King.
BRICHANTEAU (*laughing*).
Then it's no wonder that the King is sad.
BOUCHAVANNES (*laughing*).
Great fun he makes, this rabid cardinalist!
L'ANGELY (*standing*).
Be careful, gentlemen! This ministerIs mighty. A great mower, he! He makesGreat seas of blood, and then he covers themWith his red cloak and nothing more is said. [*Silence.*
GASSÉ.
Good faith!
ROCHEBARON.
I'm blessed if I shall stir!
BRICHANTEAU.
BesideThis jester Pluto was a funny man!
[*A crowd of people enter from the streets and houses, and spread over the Square. In the center appears* THE TOWN-CRIER *on horseback, with four Town-servants in livery, one of whom blows the trumpet, while the other beats the drum.*
GASSÉ.
What are these people doing? Ah, the crier!Well, paternosters are in order now!
BRICHANTEAU (*to a juggler with a monkey on his back, who has joined the crowd*).
Which one of you shows off the other, friend?
MONTPESAT (*to* ROCHEBARON).
I hope our packs of cards are still complete.
[*Indicating the four Servants in livery.*
It looks as though these knaves were stolen thence.
TOWN-CRIER (*in a nasal tone of voice*).
Peace, citizens!
BRICHANTEAU (*low to* GASSÉ).
He has a wicked look.His voice wears out his nose more than his mouth!
TOWN-CRIER.
"Ordinance: Louis, by the Grace of God—"
BOUCHAVANNES (*low to* BRICHANTEAU).
Cloak *fleur-de-lis* concealing Richelieu!
L'ANGELY.
Attention!
TOWN-CRIER (*continuing*).
"King of France and of Navarre—"
BRICHANTEAU (*low to* BOUCHAVANNES).
A fine name, which no minister e'er hoards.
TOWN-CRIER (*continuing*).
"Know all men by these presents, we greet you!"
[*He salutes assembly.*
Having considered that all kings desiredAnd have tried to abolish dueling,But yet, in spite of edicts signed by them,The evil has increased in great degree,We ordain and decree that from this timeAll duelists who rob us of our subjects,Whether but one of them or both

survive,Be brought for punishment unto our court,And commoner or noble shall be hanged.In order to give force to this edictWe here renounce our right of pardon forThis crime. It is our gracious pleasure."—Signed, LOUIS; and lower—RICHELIEU.

[*Indignation among the nobles.*

BRICHANTEAU.

What's this?We are to hang up like Barabbas!

BOUCHAVANNES.

We?Tell me the name of any place which holdsA rope by which to hang a nobleman!

TOWN-CRIER (*continuing*).

"We, provost, that all men may know these facts,Command this edict to be hung up onThe Square."

[*The two Servants attach a great placard to an iron gallows protruding from the wall on the right.*

GASSÉ.

'Tis the edict they ought to hang!Well done!

BOUCHAVANNES (*shaking his head*).

Yes, Count; while waiting for the headWhich shall defy it.

[THE TOWN-CRIER *exits; the crowd retires.* SAVERNY *enters. It begins to grow dark.*

SCENE II

The same. MARQUIS DE SAVERNY

BRICHANTEAU (*going to* SAVERNY).

Cousin Saverny,I hope you've found the man who rescued you.

SAVERNY.

No; I have searched the city through in vain.The robbers, the young man, and Marion—They have all faded from me like a dream.

BRICHANTEAU.

You must have seen him when he brought you back,Like a good Christian, from those infidels.

SAVERNY.

The first thing that he did was to throw downThe lamp.

GASSÉ.

That's strange!

BRICHANTEAU.

You'd recognize him ifYou met him?

SAVERNY.

No; I didn't see his face.

BRICHANTEAU.

What is his name?

SAVERNY.

Didier.

ROCHEBARON.

That's no man's name!That is a bourgeois name.

SAVERNY.

It doesn't matter.Didier is this man's name. There are great menWho have been conquerors and bear grand names,But they've no greater hearts than this man had.I had six robbers! He had Marion!He left her, and saved me. My debt's immense!This debt I mean to pay. I tell you all:I'll pay it with the last drop of my blood!

VILLAC.

Since when do you pay debts?

SAVERNY (*proudly*).

I've always paidThose debts which can be paid with blood.Blood is the only change I carry, sir!

[*It is quite dark; the windows in the city are lighted one by one; a lamplighter enters and lights a street-lamp above the edict and goes out. The little door through which* MARION *and* DIDIER *disappeared is re-opened.* DIDIER *comes forth dreamily, walking slowly, his arms folded.*

SCENE III

The same. DIDIER

DIDIER (*coming slowly from the back; no one sees or hears him*).

Marquis de Saverny! I would like muchTo see that fool who looked at her so hard.I have him on my mind.

BOUCHAVANNES (*to SAVERNY, who is talking with Brichanteau*).

Saverny!

DIDIER (*aside*).

Ah,That is my man!

[*He advances slowly, his eyes fixed on the noblemen, and sits down at a table placed under the street-lamp, which lights up the edict.*L'ANGELY, *motionless and silent, is a few steps distant.*

BOUCHAVANNES (*to SAVERNY, who turns around*).

You know about the edict?

SAVERNY.

Which one?

BOUCHAVANNES.

Commanding us to give up duels.

SAVERNY.

It is most wise.

BRICHANTEAU.

Hanging's the penalty.

SAVERNY.

You must be jesting. Commoners are hanged,Not nobles.

BRICHANTEAU (*showing the placard*).

Read it for yourself. It's there,Upon the wall.

SAVERNY (*perceiving DIDIER*).

That sallow face can readFor me.

[*To DIDIER, elevating his voice.*

Ho! man there with the cloak! My friend!Good fellow![*To BRICHANTEAU.*] Brichanteau, he must be deaf.

DIDIER (*slowly lifting his head, without taking his eyes from him*).

You spoke to me?

SAVERNY.

I did! In fair return,Read that placard which hangs above your head.

DIDIER.

I?

SAVERNY.

You—if you can spell the alphabet.

DIDIER (*rising*).

It is the edict threatening duelistsWith gallows, be they nobles or plebeians.

SAVERNY.

No, you mistake, my friend. You ought to knowA nobleman was never born to hang,And in this world, where we claim all our rights,Plebeians are the gallows' only prey.

[*To the noblemen.*

These commoners are rude.[*To DIDIER, with malice.*] You don't read well;Perhaps you are near-sighted. Lift your hat,'Twill give you more light. Take it off.

DIDIER (*overthrowing the table which is in front of him*).

Beware!You have insulted me! I've read for you;I claim my recompense! I'll have it, too!I want your blood, I want your head, Marquis!

SAVERNY (*smiling*).

We must be fitted to our station, sir.I judge him commoner, he scents marquisIn me.

DIDIER.

Marquis and commoner can fight.What do you say to mixing up our blood?

SAVERNY.

You go too fast, and fighting is not all.I am Gaspard, Marquis de Saverny.

DIDIER.

What does that matter?

SAVERNY.

15

Here my seconds are!The Count de Gassé, noble family,And Count de Villac, family La Teuillade,From which house comes the Marquis d'Aubusson.Are you of noble blood?

DIDIER.

What matters that?I am a foundling left at a church door.I have no name; but in its place, I've blood,To give you in exchange for yours!

SAVERNY.

That, sir,Is not enough; but as a foundling, youMay claim the right, because you might be noble.It is a better thing to lift a vassalThan to degrade a peer. You may command me!Choose your hour, sir.

DIDIER.

Immediately!

SAVERNY.

Agreed!You're no usurper, that is clear.

DIDIER.

A sword!

SAVERNY.

You have no sword? The devil! that is bad.You might be thought a man of low descent.Will you have mine?

[*Offers his sword to* DIDIER.

Well tempered and obedient!

[L'ANGELY *rises, draws his sword and presents it to* DIDIER.

L'ANGLEY.

No; for a foolish deed, you'd better takeA fool's sword! You are brave! You'll honor it![*Maliciously.*] And in return, to bring me luck, pray letMe cut a piece from off the hanging-rope!

DIDIER (*bitterly, taking sword*).

I will.

[*To* THE MARQUIS.

Now God have mercy on the good!

BRICHANTEAU (*jumping with delight*).

A duel—excellent!

SAVERNY (*to* DIDIER*).*

Where shall we fight?

DIDIER.

Beneath the street-lamp.

GASSÉ.

Gentlemen, you're mad!You cannot see. You'll put your eyes out.

DIDIER.

Humph!There's light enough to cut each other's throat.

SAVERNY.

Well said!

VILLAC.

You can see nothing.

DIDIER.

That's enough!Each sword is lightning flashing in the dark.Come, Marquis!

[*Both throw off their cloaks, take off their hats with which they salute each other, throwing them afterward on the ground. Then they draw their swords.*

SAVERNY.

At your service, sir.

DIDIER.

Now! *Garde!*

[*They cross swords and fence, silently and furiously. Suddenly the small door opens,* MARION *in a white dress appears.*

SCENE IV
The same. MARION

MARION.

What is this noise?

[*Perceiving* DIDIER *under the lamp.*]

Didier![*To the combatants.*] Stop![*They continue.*] Ho! The guard!

SAVERNY.

Who is this woman?

DIDIER (*turning*).

Heaven!

BOUCHAVANNES (*running, to* SAVERNY).

All is lost!That woman's cry went through the town.I saw the archers' rapiers flash.

[*The Archers with torches enter.*

BRICHANTEAU (*to* SAVERNY).

Seem dead,Or you will be so!

SAVERNY (*falling down*).

Ah!

[*Low to* BRICHANTEAU, *who bends over him.*

Oh, damn these stones.

[DIDIER, *who thinks he has killed him, pauses.*

CAPTAIN OF THE DISTRICT.

Hold! In the King's name!

BRICHANTEAU (*to the noblemen*).

We must save the Marquis.He's a dead man if he is caught.

[*The noblemen surround* SAVERNY.

CAPTAIN OF THE DISTRICT.

Zounds, sirs!To fight a duel 'neath the very lightOf the edict is bold indeed![*To* DIDIER.] Give upYour sword.

[*The Archers seize* DIDIER, *who stands apart, and disarm him.* THE CAPTAIN *indicates* SAVERNY *stretched upon the ground and surrounded by the noblemen.*

That other man with dull eyes, whoIs he? What is his name?

BRICHANTEAU.

His name's Gaspard,Marquis de Saverny, and he is dead.

CAPTAIN OF THE DISTRICT.

Dead, is he? Then his trouble's over. Good!This dead man's worth more than the other.

MARION (*frightened*).

What!

CAPTAIN OF THE DISTRICT (*to* DIDIER).

The whole affair rests now with you, sir. Come!

[*The Archers lead* DIDIER *off on one side, the noblemen carry*SAVERNY *off on the other.*

DIDIER (*to* MARION, *who is motionless from horror*).

Forget me, Marion. Good-by! [*They exit.*

SCENE V

MARION, L'ANGELY

MARION (*rushing to detain him*).

Didier!What do you mean? Good-by? Why this good-by?Wherefore forget you?

[*The Soldiers push her off; she approaches* L'ANGELY *with anguish.*

Is he lost for this?What did he do? What will they do to him?

L'ANGELY (*takes her hand and leads her in silence before the edict*).

Read this!

MARION (*reads, and starts back with horror*).

My God! Just God! Condemned to death!They've taken him away. To kill him! Oh,I brought this ruin on him with my cries!I called for help, but my unhappy voiceFound death in the dark streets and brought her here.Impossible! A duel is no crime!

[*To* L'ANGELY.

They'll not kill him for that?

L'ANGELY.

I think they will.

17

MARION.
He can escape!
L'ANGELY.
The prison walls are high!
MARION.
I've brought this crime upon him with my sins.God strikes him for my sake! My
Didier! love![*To* L'ANGELY.] Nothing on earth seemed good enough for him!A prison cell—
my God! Death! Torture too!
L'ANGELY.
Perhaps! It all depends—
MARION.
I'll find the King!He has a royal heart; he pardons.
L'ANGELY.
Yes,The King does, not the Cardinal.
MARION.
Then, what—What can I do?
L'ANGELY.
A capital offense,Nothing can save him from the fatal rope.
MARION.
Oh, grief![*To* L'ANGELY.] You freeze my blood, sir. Who are you?
L'ANGELY.
I'm the King's jester!
MARION.
Oh, my Didier, love,I'm lost, unworthy; but what God can doWith a weak woman's
hands, I'll show to you.Go on, my love; I follow!
[*She goes out on the side from which* DIDIER *left.*
L'ANGELY (*alone*).
God knows where!
[*Picking up the sword which* DIDIER *left on the ground.*
Among all these, who'd think I was the fool?
[*He goes out.*

ACT III
THE COMEDY

SCENE.—*The Castle of Nangis. A park in the style of Henry IV. In the background on an
elevation, the Castle of Nangis, part new, part old, is visible. The old, a castle-keep with arches and turrets:
the new, a large brick house with corners of wrought stone, and pointed roof. The large door of the castle-keep
is hung with black: from afar one distinguishes a coat-of-arms—that of the families of Nangis and of
Saverny*

SCENE I

M. DE LAFFEMAS, *undress costume of a magistrate of the period.*MARQUIS DE SAVERNY,
disguised as an officer of the Regiment of Anjou; with black mustache and imperial, and a plaster on the eye
LAFFEMAS.
Then you were present, sir, at the attack?
SAVERNY (*pulling his mustache*).
I was his comrade: had that honor, sir!But he is dead!
LAFFEMAS.
The Marquis de Saverny?
SAVERNY.
Yes, from a thrust in tierce, which burst the doublet,Then carved its cruel way
between the ribsThrough to the chest and to the liver, which,As you well know, makes
blood. The wound was fearful.'Twas horrible to see!
LAFFEMAS.
He died at once?
SAVERNY.
Almost. His agony was short. I watchedThe spasm follow frenzy; tetanosThen came,
and after opisthotonosThere followed improstathonos.

18

LAFFEMAS.
The deuce!
SAVERNY.
So that I calculate 'tis false to sayThe blood passes the jugular. PequetAnd learned men should be condemned when theyDissect live dogs to study 'bout the lungs.
LAFFEMAS.
The poor marquis is dead.
SAVERNY.
A thrust is fatal.
LAFFEMAS.
You are a doctor, sir, of medicine?
SAVERNY.
No.
LAFFEMAS.
You have studied it?
SAVERNY.
Somewhat.In Aristotle.
LAFFEMAS.
You can talk it well!
SAVERNY.
Faith! I've a most malicious sort of heart.I like destruction; find delight in evil;I love to kill! So that I thought I'd beA soldier or a doctor, sir, at twenty.But I hesitated long, and finallyI chose the sword. It's not so sure, but twiceAs quick. There was a time, I will confess,I longed to be a poet or an actor,Or an exhibitor of bears—but then,I like dinner and supper every day.A plague upon the poetry and bears!
LAFFEMAS.
With this hope in your mind you studied verse?
SAVERNY.
A little bit, in Aristotle. Yes—
LAFFEMAS.
The Marquis knew you?
SAVERNY.
He knew me as wellAs a lieutenant knows an upstart soldier.I belonged to Monsieur de Caussade first,Who gave me to the Marquis' colonel. PoorThe present, but we do the best we can!They made me officer—I'm worth as muchAs any, and I wear a black mustache.That is my history.
LAFFEMAS.
They sent you hereTo notify the uncle?
SAVERNY.
Yes; I cameWith Brichanteau, the cousin, and the corpse.He will be buried here—where, if he'd lived,He would have had his wedding!
LAFFEMAS.
Tell me howThe old Marquis de Nangis bore the news.
SAVERNY.
With calmness, without tears.
LAFFEMAS.
He loved him though?
SAVERNY.
As much as we love life. Having no childrenOf his own he had but this one passion—His nephew, whom he dearly loved, althoughThey had not seen each other for five years.

[*In the background, the old* MARQUIS DE NANGIS *passes; white hair, pale countenance, arms folded across his breast, dress of the day of Henry IV.: deep mourning; the star and the ribbon of the order of the Holy Ghost. He walks slowly; nine guards in three rows follow; they are dressed in mourning, their halberds on their right shoulder, their muskets on their left; they keep within a short distance, stopping when he stops, and continuing when he continues.*

LAFFEMAS (*watching him pass*).

Poor man!

[*He goes to the back and follows* THE MARQUIS *with his eyes.*

SAVERNY (*aside*).

My good old uncle!

[BRICHANTEAU *enters and goes to* SAVERNY.

SCENE II

The same. BRICHANTEAU

BRICHANTEAU.

Ah! two words![*Laughing.*] He's looking pretty well for a dead man!

SAVERNY (*low, indicating* THE MARQUIS, *who passes*).

Why do you make me grieve him, Brichanteau?I think we might explain it to him now.Oh, let me try.

BRICHANTEAU.

No; God forbid, my friend!His grief must be sincere; he must weep much.His woe is one good half of your disguise.

SAVERNY.

Poor uncle!

BRICHANTEAU.

He will find it out ere long.

SAVERNY.

If sorrow has not killed him, then joy will.These shocks are dangerous to such old men.

BRICHANTEAU.

It must be done!

SAVERNY.

I cannot bear to hearHim laugh so bitterly, then weep; then keepSo still! I hate to see him kiss that coffin.

BRICHANTEAU.

Yes—a fine coffin with no corpse in it!

SAVERNY.

But I am dead and bleeding in his heart.The corpse lies there.

LAFFEMAS (*coming back*).

Alas, the poor old man!His eyes show plainly how he's suffering!

BRICHANTEAU (*low to* SAVERNY).

Who is that surly-looking man in black?

SAVERNY (*with gesture of ignorance*).

Some friend who's living at the castle?

BRICHANTEAU (*low*).

CrowsAre also black and love the smell of death.Keep silence more than ever. 'Tis a faceThat's treacherous and evil; it would makeA madman prudent.

[THE MARQUIS DE NANGIS *re-enters; he is still absorbed in a deep reverie. He walks slowly, does not appear to notice any one, and seats himself upon a bank of turf.*

SCENE III

The same. MARQUIS DE NANGIS

LAFFEMAS (*approaching* THE MARQUIS).

Marquis, we've lost much.He was a rare man; would have comfortedYour old age. I mingle my tears with yours.Young, handsome, good, naught more could be desired;Obeying God, respecting women, strong;Just in his actions, sensible in speech,A perfect nobleman, whom all revere!To die so young! Most cruel fate! Alas!

[THE MARQUIS *lets his head fall on his hands.*

SAVERNY (*low to* BRICHANTEAU).

The devil take this funeral discourse!These praises but augment the old man's grief.Console him, you; Show him the other side.

BRICHANTEAU (*to* LAFFEMAS).

You are mistaken, sir. I was in theSame grade. A bad comrade, this Saverny—A
shiftless fellow, growing worse each day.Courageous! Every man is brave at twenty;His death
is nothing much to boast about.

LAFFEMAS.

A duel! Surely, that is no great crime.

[*Banteringly to* BRICHANTEAU, *pointing to his sword.*

You are an officer?

BRICHANTEAU (*in the same tone, pointing to* LAFFEMAS'S *wig*).

A magistrate?

SAVERNY (*low*).

Go on!

BRICHANTEAU.

He was capricious, thankless, andA liar: not worth any real regret.He went to church,
but just to ogle girls.He was a gallant, a mere libertine,A fool!

SAVERNY (*low*).

Good! good!

BRICHANTEAU.

Intractable and stubborn;Rude to his officers. As to good looks,He had lost his; he
limped, had a large wenUpon his eye; from blonde had turned to red,And from round-
shouldered had become hump-backed.

SAVERNY (*low*).

Enough!

BRICHANTEAU.

He gambled—every one knows that.He would have staked his soul on dice. I'll
wagerThat cards had eaten up his property.His fortune galloped faster every night.

SAVERNY (*low, pulling his sleeve*).

Enough! Good God! Your consolation isToo strong.

LAFFEMAS.

To speak so ill of a dead friend!Unpardonable!

BRICHANTEAU (*indicating* SAVERNY).

Ask this gentleman!

SAVERNY.

Oh, no; I beg to be excused!

LAFFEMAS (*affectionately, to the old* MARQUIS).

My lord,We'll comfort you. We have his murderer,And we will hang him. We have
kept him safe.His end is sure.

[*To* BRICHANTEAU *and* SAVERNY.

But can one understandThe Marquis? There are duels, we all know,That cannot be
avoided, but to fightWith any one named Didier—

SAVERNY (*aside*).

What? Didier?

[*The old* MARQUIS, *who has remained silent and motionless during all this scene, rises and goes out
slowly on the side opposite where he came in. His guards follow him.*

LAFFEMAS (*wiping away a tear and following him with his eyes*).

In truth, his sorrow deeply touches me.

LACKEY (*running*).

My lord!

BRICHANTEAU.

Why can't you leave your master quiet?

LACKEY.

It is the burial of the young marquis!What is the hour?

BRICHANTEAU.

You'll know it by-and-by.

LACKEY.

A few comedians have arrived here fromThe city; they beg shelter for the night.

BRICHANTEAU.

The time's ill-chosen for comedians, butThe law of hospitality holds good.Give them this barn.
[*Indicating a barn on the left.*
LACKEY (*holding a letter*).
A letter! 'Tis important![*Reading.*] For a Monsieur de Laffemas.
LAFFEMAS.
'Tis I!Give it to me!
BRICHANTEAU (*low to* SAVERNY, *who has remained thoughtful in a corner*).
Saverny, let us go!Come and arrange things for your funeral!
[*Pulling him by the sleeve.*
What is it? Are you dreaming?
SAVERNY (*aside*).
Oh, Didier!
[*They go out.*

SCENE IV

LAFFEMAS (*alone*).
The seal of State! The great seal of red wax!Come! this is business. Let me know at once![*Reading.*] "Sir Criminal Lieutenant: We make knownTo you that Didier, the assassin ofThe late Marquis Gaspard, has fled." My God!That is unfortunate! "A woman isWith him, called Marion de Lorme. We begYou to return as soon as possible."Quick! Get me horses! I, who felt so sure!Another matter spoiled for want of sense.Outrageous! Of the two, not one! One, dead!Escaped, the other! I will catch him, though!
[*He exits. Enter a troupe of strolling actors, men, women and children in character costumes. Among them are* MARION *and* DIDIER, *dressed as Spaniards.* DIDIER *wears a great felt hat and is covered with a cloak.*

SCENE V
The Comedians, MARION, DIDIER

A LACKEY (*conducting the Comedians to the barn*).
This is your lodging. You're on the estateOf the Marquis de Nangis. Behave well,Try to be quiet, for some one is dead.The burial is to-morrow. Above all,Don't mix your songs with the funereal chantsWhich will be sung for him throughout the night.
GRACIEUX (*small and hump-backed*).
We'll make less noise than do your hunting-dogsWho bark around the legs of all who pass!
LACKEY.
Dogs are not actors, my good friend.
TAILLEBRAS (*to* GRACIEUX).
Be still!You'll cause us to sleep in the open air!
[LACKEY *exits.*
SCARAMOUCHE (*to* MARION *and* DIDIER, *who until now have remained quietly apart*).
Come! let us talk. Now you belong to us.Why Monsieur fled with Madame on behind,If you are man and wife or lovers only,Escaping justice, or black sorcerersWho held Madame a prisoner, perhaps—Is not my business. What I want to knowIs what you'll act. Chimènes are best for you,Black eyes.
[MARION *makes a courtesy.*
DIDIER (*aside, indignant*).
To hear that mountebank speak thus!
SCARAMOUCHE (*to* DIDIER).
For you: if you should want a splendid part,We need a bully—a long-leggèd man,Tremendous strides, a thundering voice; and whenOrgon is robbed of wife or niece, you killThe Moor and terminate the piece. Great part!High tragedy! 'Twill suit you splendidly.
DIDIER.
Just as you please!
SCARAMOUCHE.
Good! Don't say "you" to me!I like "thou"! [*With a profound obeisance.*Blusterer, hail!

DIDIER (*aside*).

What fools!

SCARAMOUCHE (*to the other actors*).

Now eat;Then we'll rehearse our parts.

[*All enter the barn except* MARION *and* DIDIER.

SCENE VI

MARION, DIDIER; *afterward* GRACIEUX, SAVERNY, *afterward* LAFFEMAS

DIDIER (*with bitter laugh, after a long silence*).

Is't bad enough?My Marion, have I dragged you low enough?You wished to follow me? My destinyPrecipitates itself and crushes you,Bound to its wheel! What are we come to now?I told you so!

MARION (*trembling and clasping her hands*).

Do you reproach me, love?

DIDIER.

Oh, may I be accursed! Cursed first by Heaven,Then cursed 'mongst men: cursed throughout all my life;Cursed more than we are now, if a reproachShall ever leave my lips for you! What matterThough all the earth abandon me, you're mine!You are my savior, refuge, all my hope!Who duped the jailer, filed my chains for me?Who came from heaven to follow me to hell?Who was a captive with the prisoner,An exile with the fugitive? Ah, who,Who else had heart so full of love and wit,Heart to sustain, console, deliver me?Great, feeble woman, have you not saved meFrom destiny, alas! and my own soul?Had you not pity on my nature, crushed?Have you not loved one whom all others hate?

MARION (*weeping*).

It is my joy to love you—be your slave.

DIDIER.

Leave me your eyes, dear; they enrapture me!God willed, when placing soul within my flesh,A demon and an angel should guide me.Yet he was merciful; his love concealedThe demon, but the angel he revealed.

MARION.

You are my Didier, master, lord of me!

DIDIER.

Your husband, am I not?

MARION (*aside*).

Alas!

DIDIER.

What joy,When we have left this country far behind,To have you, call you wife as well as love!You will be willing?—answer.

MARION.

I will beYour sister, and my brother you shall be!

DIDIER.

Oh, no! Refuse me not that ecstasyOf knowing, in God's sight, you're mine alone!You're safe to trust my love in everything.The lover keeps you for the husband, pure!

MARION (*aside*).

Alas!

DIDIER.

If you knew how things torture me!To hear that actor talk, affront you thus!It is not least among our wretched woesTo see you mixed with jugglers such as these,A chaste, exquisite flower 'mid this filth—You, 'mongst these women steeped in infamy!

MARION.

Be prudent, Didier!

DIDIER.

God! I struggled hardAgainst my anger! He said "thou" to you,When I, your love, your husband, hardly dareFor fear of tarnishing that virgin brow—

MARION.

Be pleasant with them; it means life to you,And me as well.

DIDIER.

She's right. She's always right.Although each hour brings us increasing woe,You lavish on me love and joy and youth!How happens it these blessings come to me,When royal kingdoms were small for them—To me, who give but anguish in return?Heaven gave you—yes; but hell binds you to me.For us to merit this unequal fate,What good can I have done? What evil you?

MARION.

My only blessings come from you, my love!

DIDIER.

If you say that you think it, but it's wrong!Oh, yes, my star of destiny is bad.I know not whence I come, nor where I go.My whole horizon's dark. Love, hark to me!There's time yet; you can leave me and go back.Let me pursue the gloomy route alone.When all is ended and I'm tired out,The couch that's waiting will be cold—ice-cold,And narrow; there's not room enough for two.Go back!

MARION.

That couch, dark, and mysterious,I'll share it with you; that at least is mine.

DIDIER.

Will you not listen? Can't you understand?You're tempting Providence to cling to me!The years of anguish, love, may be so longYour sweet eyes may grow sightless, just from tears.

[MARION *lets her head fall on her hands.*

DIDIER.

I swear I draw the picture none too strong.Your future frightens me. I pity you!Go back!

MARION (*bursting into tears*).

It were more kind to kill me, Didier,Than to talk thus! [*Weeping.*] O God!

DIDIER (*taking her in his arms*).

My darling, hush!So many tears! I'd shed my blood for one.Do what you will! Come, be my destiny,My glory, life, my virtue, and my love!Answer me now. I speak! Sweet, do you hear?

[*He seats her on a bank of turf.*

MARION (*withdrawing herself from his arms*).

You've hurt me!

DIDIER (*kneeling to her*).

I, who'd gladly die for her!

MARION (*smiling through her tears*).

You made me cry, you cruel man!

DIDIER.

My beauty!

[*Sits on the bank beside her.*

Just one sweet kiss upon your forehead, pureAs is our love!

[*He kisses her forehead. They look at each other with ecstasy.*

Yes, look at me! Look thus,Look harder; look until we die of looking!

GRACIEUX (*entering*).

Dona Chimène is wanted in the barn.

[MARION *rises hastily from* DIDIER'S *side. At the same time that*GRACIEUX *enters,* SAVERNY *comes in; he stands in the background and looks attentively at* MARION *without seeing* DIDIER, *who remains sitting on the bank and is hidden by a bush.*

SAVERNY (*back, without being seen, aside*).

Faith, it is Marion! What brings her here?[*Laughing.*] Chimène!

GRACIEUX (*to* DIDIER, *who is about to follow* MARION).

Oh, no! stay there, my jealous friend,I want to tease you!

DIDIER.

Devil take you!

MARION (*low to* DIDIER).

Hush!Restrain yourself.

[DIDIER *re-seats himself; she enters the barn.*

SAVERNY (*still back, aside*).
What makes her roam the country in this fashion?Can he be the gallant who succored
me?Who saved my life? Didier! It is indeed!
LAFFEMAS (*enters in traveling costume, and salutes* SAVERNY).
I take my leave, sir!
SAVERNY (*bowing*).
You are going away?
[*He laughs.*
LAFFEMAS.
What makes you laugh?
SAVERNY.
A very silly thing.I'll tell you. Guess whom I have recognizedAmong those jugglers
who have just arrived.
LAFFEMAS.
Among those jugglers?
SAVERNY (*laughing still more*).
Yes. Marion de Lorme!
LAFFEMAS (*with a start*).
Marion de Lorme!
DIDIER (*who has been looking at them fixedly all the time*).
Hein? [*He half rises from the bank.*
SAVERNY (*still laughing*).
I would like to sendThat news to Paris. Are you going there?
LAFFEMAS.
I am, and I will spread the news, trust me!But are you sure you recognize her?
SAVERNY.
Sure?Hurrah for France! We know our Marion.
[*Feeling in his pocket.*
I think I have her portrait—tender pledgeOf love! She had it done by the King's
painter.
[*Giving* LAFFEMAS *a locket.*
Look and compare them.
[*Indicating the barn door.*
See her, through that door,In Spanish costume, with green petticoat.
LAFFEMAS (*looking from the locket to the barn*).
'Tis she—Marion de Lorme! [*Aside.*] I have him now!
[*To* SAVERNY.] She must have a companion 'mongst these men.
SAVERNY.
It's likely. Such fair ladies are not prudes,And seldom travel round the world alone.
LAFFEMAS (*aside*).
I'll guard this door. It will go hard, indeed,If I can't capture that false actor here.He's
taken now—no doubt of that! [*Goes out.*
SAVERNY (*watches the exit of* LAFFEMAS: *aside*).
I thinkI've done a foolish thing.
[*Taking* GRACIEUX *aside, who all this time has stood in a corner gesticulating and running over
his lines: in a whisper.*
Who is that ladySitting within the shadow there?
[*Indicating the door of the barn.*
GRACIEUX.
Chimène?[*Solemnly.*] My lord, I do not know her name. Ask him,This lord, her noble
friend.
[*Exits on the side of the park.*
SCENE VII
DIDIER, SAVERNY
SAVERNY (*turning toward* DIDIER).

This gentleman? Tell me— 'Tis strange how hard he looks at me! Upon my soul, 'tis
he! My man! [*Loud to* DIDIER.] If you Were not in prison, I should say that you Resemble a—
DIDIER.
And if you were not dead, I'd say That you had the exact appearance of—His blood
be on his head!—a man whom two Short words of mine put in a tomb.
SAVERNY.
Hush! You Are Didier!
DIDIER.
Marquis Gaspard, you!
SAVERNY.
'Twas you Who were somewhere, a certain night! 'Tis you To whom I owe my life!
[*He opens his arms.* DIDIER *draws back.*
DIDIER.
Excuse surprise! I felt so sure I took it back.
SAVERNY.
Not so! You saved me—did not kill me! Let me know What I can do for you. Do you
desire A second—brother—a lieutenant? Speak! What will you have—my blood, my wealth,
my soul?
DIDIER.
Not any of those things. That portrait there!
[SAVERNY *gives him the portrait; he looks at it, speaking with bitterness.*
Yes, there's her brow, her black eyes, her white neck; Above all, there's her candid
glance! How like!
SAVERNY.
You think so?
DIDIER.
This was made for you, you say?
SAVERNY (*bowing, and making an affirmative sign*).
It was! But now 'tis you whom she prefers, You whom she loves and chooses 'mongst
us all. You are a happy man.
DIDIER (*with loud and mocking laugh*).
Yes! Am I not?
SAVERNY.
Accept my compliments; she's a good girl, And loves no one but men of family. Of
such a mistress one can well be proud! It's honorable, and it gives one style. 'Tis in good taste.
If men ask who you are They say, "Beloved of Marion de Lorme."
[DIDIER *gives him back the portrait; he refuses it.*
No, keep the portrait; since the lady's yours, It should belong to you. Keep it, I pray.
DIDIER.
I thank you! [*Puts it in his breast.*
SAVERNY.
She is charming in that dress. So you are my successor! One might say, As King Louis
succeeded Pharamond. The Brissacs, both of them, supplanted me. [*Laughing.*] Then, yes, the
Cardinal himself came next, Then little D'Effiat, then the three Sainte-Mesmes, The four
Argenteans! In her heart you'll find The best society. [*Laughing.*] A little numerous.
DIDIER (*aside*).
My God!
SAVERNY.
Tell me about it some time. Now, To be quite frank with you, I pass for dead, And in
the morning shall be buried. You Must have escaped police and seneschals. Your Marion can
manage everything! You joined a strolling company by chance; What a delightful history!
DIDIER.
Yes, true It is a history!
SAVERNY.
To get you out She probably made love to all the jailers.
DIDIER (*in a voice of thunder*).

26

Do you think that?

SAVERNY.

You are not jealous—what?Oh, joke incredible!—of Marion!A man jealous of Marion! The poor child!Don't go and scold her!

DIDIER.

Have no fear. [*Aside.*] The angel—It was a demon! Oh, my God!

[*Enter* LAFFEMAS *and* GRACIEUX. DIDIER *goes out;* SAVERNY *follows him.*

SCENE VIII

LAFFEMAS, GRACIEUX

GRACIEUX (*to* LAFFEMAS).

My lord,I do not understand you![*Aside.*] Humph! A costumeOf Alcaid and a figure of police;Small eyes, adorned with big eyebrows! I thinkHe plays the part of Alguazil in thisLocality.

LAFFEMAS (*pulling out his purse*).

My friend!

GRACIEUX (*drawing near, low to* LAFFEMAS).

My lord—I see!Chimène has interested you. You wishTo know—

LAFFEMAS (*low, smiling*).

Who is her Roderick?

GRACIEUX.

You meanHer lover?

LAFFEMAS.

Yes!

GRACIEUX.

Who groans beneath her spell?

LAFFEMAS (*impatiently*).

There's one?

GRACIEUX.

Of course!

LAFFEMAS (*approaching him eagerly*).

Then show him to me, quick!

GRACIEUX (*with profound obeisance*).

It's I, my lord. I'm mad about her!

LAFFEMAS.

You!

[LAFFEMAS, *disappointed, turns away with annoyance; then he comes back and shakes his purse in* GRACIEUX'S *eyes and ears.*

Know you the sound of ducats?

GRACIEUX.

Heavenly tones!

LAFFEMAS (*aside*).

I've got my Didier![*To* GRACIEUX.] Do you see this purse?

GRACIEUX.

How much!

LAFFEMAS.

Gold ducats—twenty!

GRACIEUX.

Humph!

LAFFEMAS (*jingling the gold in his face*).

Will you?

GRACIEUX (*grabbing the purse from him*).

Most certainly!

[*With theatrical tone to* LAFFEMAS, *who listens anxiously.*

My lord, if your back boreJust in the center a great hump, as bigAs is your belly, and if those two bagsWere filled with louis, sequins, and doubloons,In that case—

LAFFEMAS (*eagerly*).

27

Well, what would you do?
GRACIEUX (*putting the purse into his pocket*).
I'd takeThe whole of it, and I would say—
[*With profound obeisance.*
I thank you;You are a gentleman!
LAFFEMAS (*aside, furious*).
Plague on the monkey!
GRACIEUX (*aside, laughing*).
The devil take the cat!
LAFFEMAS (*aside*).
They have agreedOn what to do, if any one suspects.'Tis a conspiracy. They'll all be
dumb;Accursed gypsy devils!
[*To* GRACIEUX *who is going away.*
Give me backMy purse!
GRACIEUX (*turning around, with tragic tone*).
What do you take me for, my lord?What will the world think of us, pray, if
youPropose and I agree to anythingSo infamous as sell for gold a life,My soul? [*Turns to go.*
LAFFEMAS.
That's as you please; but give me backMy money!
GRACIEUX.
No, I keep my honor, sir,And we have no accounts to settle.
[*He salutes him and re-enters barn.*

SCENE IX

LAFFEMAS (*alone*).
Humph!The wretched juggler! Pride in such base souls!If you some day should fall
into my handsUnoccupied with better sort of game—But this will not find Didier! Now, I
can'tTake all this crowd and put them to the torture.This is worse work than hunting needles
inA haystack. Faith! a chemist's crucibleBewitched I ought to have, which, eating upThe lead
and copper, would reveal at lastThe golden ingot hid by much alloy.Go to the Cardinal
without my prize?
[*Striking his brow.*
That's it! The clever thought! Oh, joy! He's mine!
[*Calling through the barn door.*
Ho, gentlemen, comedians! one word, please.
[*The actors crowd out of the barn.*

SCENE X

The same. Comedians, among them MARION and DIDIER; afterwardSAVERNY,
afterward MARQUIS DE NANGIS

SCARAMOUCHE (*to* LAFFEMAS).
What do you want with us?
LAFFEMAS.
Without preamble:My lord the Cardinal commissioned meTo find good actors, if
there may be suchWithin the provinces, to act the playsWhich he constructs in hours of
leisure whenAllowed by State affairs. In spite of careAnd earnest thought, his theater
declines,And is no credit to a cardinal-duke.
[*All the actors press eagerly forward.* SAVERNY *enters, and watches the scene with curiosity.*
GRACIEUX (*aside, counting his money*).
Twelve only! He said twenty. The old scamp!He's robbed me!
LAFFEMAS.
Let each one repeat some scene,That I may know your talents and may
choose.[*Aside.*] If he gets out of that, this Didier's sharp.[*Aloud.*] Are you all here?
[MARION *stealthily approaches* DIDIER *and tries to lead him off.*
GRACIEUX (*going up to them*).
Come with the others—you!
MARION.
Oh, heaven!

[DIDIER *leaves her and joins the actors; she follows him.*
GRACIEUX.

You're in luck to be with us.To have new clothes, get every day a feast,To speak the Cardinal's verses every night,A happy lot!

[*All the actors take their places before* LAFFEMAS. MARION *and* DIDIER*among them.* DIDIER *does not look at* MARION*; his eyes are bent on the ground; his arms are folded underneath his cloak.* MARION *watches him anxiously.*

GRACIEUX (*at head of troupe, aside*).

Who would have thought this crowRecruited actors for the Cardinal?

LAFFEMAS (*to* GRACIEUX).

First you. What do you play?

GRACIEUX (*with a low bow and a pirouette which shows off his hump*).

I'm called the SylphAmong the troupe. This piece I know the best.

[*He sings.*

"On the bald heads of magistrates,Enormous wigs are spread.Out of that fleece, in due time, comeChains, gallows, tortures dread.Whenever one called presidentShall shake his bigger head.

"Let any barber, strolling fool,Wash, powder, and pomadeThe hair which bald heads steal from beards,Let them be combed and frayedIn shape of a right gorgeous wig—Your magistrate is made.

"The lawyer is a sea of wordsHurled wildly at the bench.A killing kind of mixing upOf Latin and bad French—"

LAFFEMAS (*interrupting him*).

You sing so false, you'd make an eagle sick.Be still!

GRACIEUX (*laughing*).

I may sing false—the song is true!

LAFFEMAS (*to* SCARAMOUCHE).

It's your turn now.

SCARAMOUCHE (*bowing*).

I'm Scaramouche, my lord!"The Lady of Honor," sir, I open thus.

[*Declaiming.*

"'Naught is so fine,' said once a Queen of Spain,'As bishop at the altar, soldier inThe field, unless it is a girl in bed,Or robber on the gallows—'"

[LAFFEMAS *interrupts* SCARAMOUCHE *with a gesture and signs to*TAILLEBRAS *to speak.* TAILLEBRAS *makes a profound obeisance, then draws himself up.*

TAILLEBRAS (*with emphasis*).

As for me,Sir, I am Taillebras. From Thibet, sir,I come; I've punished the great Khan, I've capturedThe Mogul—

LAFFEMAS.

Choose something else—

[*Low to* SAVERNY, *who stands beside him.*

A beauty,Eh, this Marion!

TAILLEBRAS.

It is one of our best.If you prefer, I will be Charlemagne,The Emperor of the West.

[*Declaiming with emphasis.*

"Strange destiny!O Heaven, I appeal to you! Bear witnessUnto my woe. I must despoil myself,Surrender my beloved one to another.I must endow my rival, fill his heartWith joy, while my poor stomach stings with grief.Thus, birds, you can no more perch in the woods;Thus, flies, you can no more buzz in the fields;Thus, sheep, you can no longer wear your wool;Thus, bulls, you can no longer raze the plains."

LAFFEMAS.

Good![*To* SAVERNY.] Listen, the fine verses! "Bradamante"By Garnier; what a poet![*To* MARION.] 'Tis your turn,My beauty. First, your name.

MARION (*trembling*).

I am Chimène!

LAFFEMAS.

Indeed! Chimène? Then you must have a lover.He has killed a man in duel—
MARION (*terrified*).
Oh, heaven!
LAFFEMAS (*maliciously*).
I've a good memory. If one escapes—
MARION (*aside*).
Great heaven!
LAFFEMAS.
Come! Now let us hear your scene
MARION (*half turned toward* DIDIER).
"Since to arrest you in this fatal courseYour life and honor are of no avail,If ever I have loved you, Roderick,Defend yourself to save me from Don Sancho.Fight valiantly against the fearful fateWhich must surrender me to one I hate.Shall I say more? Go; your defense shall beYour right to force my duty, seal my lips!If love for me still in your brave heart lies,Go win this combat, for Chimène is prize."
[LAFFEMAS *rises gallantly and kisses her hand.* MARION *is pale; she looks at* DIDIER, *who remains motionless with eyes on the ground.*
LAFFEMAS.
No voice but yours could take so firm a holdUpon the secret fibers of our heart.You are adorable.[*To* SAVERNY.] You can't denyCorneille is not worth Garnier, after all.'Tis true, his verses have a finer ringSince he's belonged unto the Cardinal-Duke.[*To* MARION.] What a complexion! What fine eyes! Good God!This is no place for you! You're buried here.Sit down!
[*He sits and makes sign to* MARION *to sit beside him; she draws back.*
MARION (*low to* DIDIER, *with anguish*).
For God's sake, let me stay with you!
LAFFEMAS (*smiling*).
Come sit by me, I say!
[DIDIER *repulses* MARION, *who staggers terrified to the bench where*LAFFEMAS *sits, and falls upon it.*
MARION (*aside*).
'Tis horrible!
LAFFEMAS (*smiling at Marion, with an air of reproach*).
At last![*To* DIDIER.] Now, sir, your turn. What is your name?
DIDIER (*with gravity*).
My name is Didier!
MARION, LAFFEMAS, SAVERNY.
Didier!
DIDIER (*to* LAFFEMAS, *who laughs triumphantly*).
Yes, you canSend all of them away. You've got your prey.Your prisoner himself takes up his chain.This joy has cost you a great deal of work.
MARION (*running to him*).
Didier!
DIDIER (*with a freezing look*).
Don't try to hinder me this time,Madame!
[*She starts back and falls crushed upon the bank: to* LAFFEMAS.
I've watched you creeping close to me,You demon! In your eyes I've seen that glareOf hell fire which illuminates your soul.I might have 'scaped your trap—a useless thing;But to see cunning wasted thus grieved me.Take me, and get well paid for treachery.
LAFFEMAS (*with concentrated rage, trying to laugh*).
You are not a comedian, it would seem!
DIDIER.
It's you who played the comedy.
LAFFEMAS.
Not well.But with the Cardinal I'll write a play.It is a tragedy: you have a part.
[MARION *screams with horror.* DIDIER *turns from her with contempt.*

Don't turn your head in such a lordly way.We will admire your acting, never fear!Come, recommend your soul to God, my friend.

MARION.

Ah, God!

[*At this moment* MARQUIS DE NANGIS *passes across the back of the stage, in the same attitude, with his escort of Halberdiers.* MARION'S *cry arrests him; pale and silent he turns to the characters.*

LAFFEMAS (*to* MARQUIS DE NANGIS).

Marquis, I claim your aid. Good news!Lend me your escort. The murderer escapedOur vigilance, but we've recaptured him.

MARION (*throwing herself at* LAFFEMAS'S *feet*).

Oh, pity for him!

LAFFEMAS (*with gallantry*).

At my feet, madame!'Tis I should kneel at yours.

MARION (*on her knees, clasping her hands*).

My lord the judge,Have mercy upon others, if some dayYou hope a jealous judge, more powerfulThan you are, will be merciful to you!

LAFFEMAS (*smiling*).

You're preaching us a sermon, I believe!Ah, madame, reign at balls and shine at fêtes,But do not preach us sermons. For your sake,I would do anything; but he has killed—It is a murder.

DIDIER (*to* MARION).

Rise! [MARION *rises, trembling.*You lie! it was a duel.

LAFFEMAS.

Sir!

DIDIER.

I say, you lie!

LAFFEMAS.

Have done![*To* MARION.] Blood callsFor blood; this rigor troubles me— I wish—But he has killed—killed whom? The young marquis,Gaspard de Saverny,

[*Indicating* MARQUIS DE NANGIS.

Nephew to him,That worthy old man there. A rare young lord;The greatest loss for France and for the King.Were he not dead, I do not say that I—My heart is not of stone, and if—

SAVERNY (*taking a step forward*).

The manYou think is dead is living. I am he!

[*General astonishment.*

LAFFEMAS (*starting*).

Gaspard de Saverny! A miracle!There is his coffin.

SAVERNY (*tearing off his false mustache, his plaster, and black wig*).

But he is not dead!Who recognizes me?

MARQUIS DE NANGIS (*as if awakening from a dream, starts, and with a great cry throws himself into his nephew's arms*).

Gaspard! My nephew!It is my child! [*They remain locked in each other's arms.*

MARION (*falling upon her knees and lifting her eyes to heaven*).

Didier is saved! Praise God!

DIDIER (*coldly, to* SAVERNY).

What is the use? I wished to die.

MARION (*still on her knees*).

Kind God,You have protected him!

DIDIER (*continuing, without listening to her*).

How otherwiseCould he have caught me in his trap? Think youMy spur could not have crushed the spider's webWhich he had made to catch a gnat? HenceforthI ask no other boon than death. This isNo friendly gift from you, who owe me life!

MARION.

What does he say? You must live—

LAFFEMAS.

31

All's not over.Is it certain that this is the Marquis?
MARION.
It is.
LAFFEMAS.
We must have proof of it at once.
MARION (*indicating* MARQUIS DE NANGIS, *who is still holding* SAVERNY *in his arms*).
Look at that old man, how he smiles and weeps!
LAFFEMAS.
Is that Gaspard de Saverny?
MARION.
What heartCan question such a close embrace?
MARQUIS DE NANGIS (*turning around*).
You askIf it is he—Gaspard, my son, my soul?[*To* MARION.] Did he not ask if it was
he, madame?
LAFFEMAS (*to* MARQUIS DE NANGIS).
Then you affirm that this man is your nephew?He is Gaspard de Saverny?
MARQUIS DE NANGIS (*with intensity*).
I do!
LAFFEMAS.
According to the law I do arrestGaspard de Saverny, in the King's name.Your sword!
[*Surprise and consternation among the characters.*
MARQUIS DE NANGIS.
My son!
MARION.
Oh, Heaven!
DIDIER.
Another head!Yes, two were needed. 'Tis the least, to bringThis Roman Cæsar one
head in each hand.
MARQUIS DE NANGIS.
Speak! By what right—
LAFFEMAS.
Ask my lord cardinal.All who survive a duel fall beneathThe ordinance. Give me your
sword.
DIDIER (*looking at* SAVERNY).
Rash man!
SAVERNY (*drawing his sword and presenting it to* LAFFEMAS).
'Tis here!
MARQUIS DE NANGIS (*stopping him*).
A moment! None is master hereSave me! I mete out justice high and low.Our sire the
King would be no more than guest.[*To* SAVERNY.] Give up your sword to none but me.
[SAVERNY *hands him his sword, and clasps him in his arms.*
LAFFEMAS.
In truth,That is a feudal right quite out of date.The Cardinal might blame me for it,
butI would not willingly annoy you—
DIDIER.
Wretch!
LAFFEMAS (*bowing to* MARQUIS DE NANGIS).
So I consent. You can return the favorBy loaning me your guard and prison, sir.
MARQUIS DE NANGIS (*to his Guards*).
Not so! Your sires were vassals to my sires.I forbid any one to stir a step.
LAFFEMAS (*with voice of thunder*).
My masters, hark to me: I am the judgeOf the secret tribunal, Criminal-Lieutenant to
the Cardinal. ConductThese men to prison. Four of you mount guardBefore each door.
You're all responsible.It would be rash to disobey when I commandYou to go here or there
or do a deed.If any hesitate, it is becauseHis head annoys him.

[*The Guards, terrified, drag the two prisoners off in silence,* MARQUIS DE NANGIS *turns away indignant and buries his face in his hands.*

MARION.
All is lost![*To* LAFFEMAS.] Have pity!If in your heart—
LAFFEMAS (*low to* MARION).
If you will come to-night,I'll tell you something—
MARION (*aside*).
What is it he wants?His smiles are terrible. He has a gloomy,Treacherous soul.
[*Turning with desperation to* DIDIER.
Didier!
DIDIER (*coldly*).
Farewell, madame!
MARION (*shuddering at the tone of his voice*).
What have I done? Oh, miserable woman!
[*She sinks upon the bank.*
DIDIER.
Miserable! Yes!
SAVERNY (*embraces* MARQUIS DE NANGIS, *then turns to* LAFFEMAS).
Is your pay doubledWhen you bring two heads?
LACKEY (*entering, to* MARQUIS DE NANGIS).
My lord,The funeral preparations for the MarquisAre now completed. I am sent to youTo know what hour and day the ceremonyWill be performed.
LAFFEMAS.
Come back one month from now.
[*The Guards lead off* DIDIER *and* SAVERNY.

ACT IV
THE KING

SCENE.—*Chambord. The guard-room in the Castle of Chambord*

SCENE I

DUKE DE BELLEGARDE, *rich court costume covered with embroidery and lace, the order of the Holy Ghost around his neck, and the star upon his cloak.* MARQUIS DE NANGIS, *in deep mourning and followed by his escort of Guards. Both cross the back of the hall*

DUKE DE BELLEGARDE.
Condemned?
MARQUIS DE NANGIS.
Condemned!
DUKE DE BELLEGARDE.
E'en so! The King can pardon.It is his kingly right and royal duty.Have no more fear. In heart as well as nameHe's son of Henry IV.
MARQUIS DE NANGIS.
I was his comrade.
DUKE DE BELLEGARDE.
Indeed, we spoiled full many a coat of armorFor the proud sire! Now go unto the son,Show him your gray hairs, and in lieu of prayerCry out "Ventre Saint Gris!" Let RichelieuHimself give better reason! Hide here now.
[*He opens a side door.*
He's coming soon. Do you know, to be frank,Your costume's of a style to make one laugh.
MARQUIS DE NANGIS.
Laugh at my mourning?
DUKE DE BELLEGARDE.
Ah, these coxcombs here!Old friend, stay there; you'll not have long to wait.I will dispose him 'gainst the Cardinal.I'll stamp upon the ground for signal; thenCome out.
MARQUIS DE NANGIS (*grasping his hand*).
May God repay you!

DUKE DE BELLEGARDE (*to a* MUSKETEER *who walks up and down in front of a small gilt door*).
Monsieur, pray,What does the King?
MUSKETEER.
He's working, my lord duke!
[*Lowering his voice.*
A man in black is with him.
DUKE DE BELLEGARDE (*aside*).
At this momentHe is singing a death-warrant, I believe.
[*To the old* MARQUIS, *grasping his hand.*
Be brave!
[*He conducts him to a neighboring gallery.*
While waiting for the signal, lookAt these new ceilings, they're by Primatice.
[*Both go out.* MARION, *in deep mourning, enters through the great door in the back, which opens on a staircase.*

SCENE II
MARION, *the Guards*

HALBERDIER (*to* MARION).
Madame, you cannot enter!
MARION (*advancing*).
Sir!
HALBERDIER (*placing his halberd against the door*).
I say,No entrance!
MARION (*with contempt*).
Here you turn your lance againstA woman. Elsewhere, 'tis in her defense.
MUSKETEER (*laughing, to* HALBERDIER).
Well said!
MARION (*firmly*).
I must immediately have audienceWith the Duke de Bellegarde.
HALBERDIER (*lowering his halberd, aside*).
Ah, these gallants!
MUSKETEER.
Enter, madame.
[*She enters with determined step.*
HALBERDIER (*aside, watching her from the corner of his eye*).
Well, the old duke is notAs feeble as he looks. This rendezvousWould have cost him a sojourn in the Louvre,In former times.
MUSKETEER (*making sign to* HALBERDIER *to keep still*).
The door is open.
[*The little gilt door is opened.* M. DE LAFFEMAS *comes out, holding in his hand a parchment to which a red seal hangs by strands of silk.*

SCENE III
MARION, LAFFEMAS: *gesture of surprise from both.* MARION *turns away from him with horror*
LAFFEMAS (*low, advancing slowly toward* MARION).
You!What is your errand here?
MARION.
What's yours?
LAFFEMAS (*unrolls the parchment and spreads it out before her eyes*).
Signed byThe King!
MARION (*glances at it, then buries her face in her hands*).
Good God!
LAFFEMAS (*speaking in her ear*).
Will you?
[MARION *shivers and looks him in the face; he fixes his eyes on hers: lowering his voice.*
Wilt thou?
MARION (*pushing him away*).

34

Away!Foul tempter!

LAFFEMAS (*straightening himself up, sneeringly*).

You will not!

MARION.

I have no fear!The King can pardon: 'tis the King who reigns.

LAFFEMAS.

Go try him. See what his good will is worth!

[*He turns away, then turns back: folds his arms and whispers to her.*

Beware of waiting until I refuse!

[*Exits.* DUKE DE BELLEGARDE *enters.*

SCENE IV

MARION, DUKE DE BELLEGARDE

MARION (*going toward* DUKE DE BELLEGARDE).

Here you are captain, my lord duke.

DUKE DE BELLEGARDE.

'Tis you,My beauty! [*Bowing.*Speak! What does my queen desire?

MARION.

To see the King.

DUKE DE BELLEGARDE.

When?

MARION.

Now!

DUKE DE BELLEGARDE.

This is short notice!Why?

MARION.

For something!

DUKE DE BELLEGARDE (*bursting into a laugh*).

We will send for him!How she goes on!

MARION.

Then you refuse me?

DUKE DE BELLEGARDE.

Nay!Am I not yours? Have we refused each otherAnything?

MARION.

That's very well, my lord!When shall I see the King?

DUKE DE BELLEGARDE.

After the Duke.I promise you shall see him when he passesThrough this hall. But while waiting, talk with me!Ah, little woman, are we good? In black?Lady-in-waiting you might be. You usedTo laugh so much.

MARION.

I don't laugh now.

DUKE DE BELLEGARDE.

Indeed!I think she's weeping! Marion! You?

MARION (*wiping her eyes: with firm tone*).

My lord,I want to see his Majesty at once!

DUKE DE BELLEGARDE.

For what?

MARION.

Just Heaven! For—

DUKE DE BELLEGARDE.

Is it againstThe Cardinal?

MARION.

It is!

DUKE DE BELLEGARDE (*opening the gallery for her*).

Please enter here.I put the discontented all in there;Do not come out before the signal, please.

[MARION *enters; he shuts door.*

I would have run the risk for my old friend.It costs no more to do it for them both.
[*The hall is gradually filled with Courtiers; they talk together.* DUKE DE BELLEGARDE *goes from one to the other.* L'ANGELY *enters.*

SCENE V
The same. DUKE DE BEAUPRÉAU, LAFFEMAS, VISCOUNT DE ROHAN, COUNT DE CHARNACÉ, ABBÉ DE GONDI, *and other courtiers*
DUKE DE BELLEGARDE (*to* DUKE DE BEAUPRÉAU).
Good-morning, Duke!
DUKE DE BEAUPRÉAU.
Good-morning!
DUKE DE BELLEGARDE.
Any news?
DUKE DE BEAUPRÉAU.
There's talk of a new cardinal.
DUKE DE BELLEGARDE.
Which one?The Archbishop of Arle?
DUKE DE BEAUPRÉAU.
No! Bishop of Autun.All Paris thinks he has obtained the hat.
ABBÉ DE GONDI.
'Tis his by right. He was commander ofArtillery at the siege of La Rochelle.
DUKE DE BELLEGARDE.
That's true!
L'ANGELY.
The Holy See has my approval.This one will be a cardinal accordingTo the canons.
ABBÉ DE GONDI (*laughing*).
L'Angely—the fool!
L'ANGELY (*bowing*).
My lord knows all my names.
[LAFFEMAS *enters; all the Courtiers vie with each other in paying court to him and surrounding him.* DUKE DE BELLEGARDE *watches them with vexation.*
DUKE DE BELLEGARDE (*to* L'ANGELY).
Fool, who's that manWho wears the ermine cloak?
L'ANGELY.
Whom every oneIs paying court to?
DUKE DE BELLEGARDE.
Yes. I know him not.Is he a follower of Monsieur d'Orleans?
L'ANGELY.
They would not fawn on him so much.
DUKE DE BELLEGARDE (*watching* LAFFEMAS, *who struts about*).
What airs!As if he were grandee of Spain!
L'ANGELY (*low*).
It isSir Laffemas, intendant of Champagne,Lieutenant-Criminal—
DUKE DE BELLEGARDE (*low*).
Infernal, say!He's called the Cardinal's executioner?
L'ANGELY (*still low*).
The same.
DUKE DE BELLEGARDE.
That man at Court!
L'ANGELY.
Why not? One extraTiger-cat in the menagerie!Shall I present him?
DUKE DE BELLEGARDE (*haughtily*).
Peace, you fool!
L'ANGELY.
I thinkI'd cultivate him if I were a lord.Be friendly! Unto each man comes his day.If he takes not your hand, he may your head.

[*He seeks* LAFFEMAS, *presents him to* DUKE DE BELLEGARDE, *who bows with ill-concealed displeasure.*

LAFFEMAS (*bowing*).

Sir Duke!

DUKE DE BELLEGARDE.

Sir, I am charmed—[*Aside.*] Upon my life,We're fallen low, Monsieur de Richelieu!
[LAFFEMAS *walks away.*

VISCOUNT DE ROHAN (*bursting into laughter among a group of Courtiers in the back of the hall*).

Delightful!

L'ANGELY.

What?

VISCOUNT DE ROHAN.

That Marion is here.

L'ANGELY.

Here—Marion?

VISCOUNT DE ROHAN.

We were just saying this:"Chaste Louis's guest is Marion." How rich!

L'ANGELY.

A charming piece of wit, indeed, my lord!

DUKE DE BELLEGARDE (*to* COUNT DE CHARNACÉ).

Sir wolf-hunter, have you found any prey?Is hunting good?

COUNT DE CHARNACÉ.

There's nothing! YesterdayI had great expectations, for three peasantsHad been devoured by wolves. At first I thoughtWe would find several at Chambord. I beatThe woods, but not a wolf, nor trace of one![*To* L'ANGELY.] Fool, know you anything that's gay?

L'ANGELY.

Nothing,My lord, except two men will soon be hangedAt Beaugency for dueling.

ABBÉ DE GONDI.

So little,Bah! [*The small gilt door is opened.*

AN USHER.

The King!

[THE KING *enters; he is in black, his eyes are cast down. The order of the Holy Ghost is on his doublet and his cloak. Hat on his head. The Courtiers all uncover and range themselves, silently, in two rows. The Guards lower their pikes and present muskets.*

SCENE VI

The same. THE KING. THE KING *enters slowly, passes through the crowd of Courtiers, without lifting his head, stops at front of stage, and stands for several instants absorbed and silent. The Courtiers retire to the back of the hall*

THE KING.

All things move on from bad to worse. Yes, all!

[*To Courtiers, nodding his head.*

God keep you, gentlemen!

[*He throws himself into a large armchair and sighs profoundly.*

I have slept ill!

[*To* DUKE DE BELLEGARDE.

My lord!

DUKE DE BELLEGARDE (*advancing with three profound salutations*).

The time for sleeping, sire, is past.

THE KING (*eagerly*).

True, Duke! The State is rushing to destructionWith giant strides!

DUKE DE BELLEGARDE.

'Tis guided by a handBoth strong and wise.

THE KING.

He bears a heavy burden,Our good lord cardinal!

DUKE DE BELLEGARDE.

Sire!

THE KING.

He is old.I ought to spare him, but I have enoughTo do with living, without reigning!

DUKE DE BELLEGARDE.

Sire,The Cardinal's not old!

THE KING.

Pray, tell me frankly—No one is watching or is listening here—What do you think of him?

DUKE DE BELLEGARDE.

Of whom, sire?

THE KING.

Him!

DUKE DE BELLEGARDE.

His Eminence?

THE KING.

Of course!

DUKE DE BELLEGARDE.

My dazzled eyesCan hardly fix themselves—

THE KING.

Is that your frankness?There is no cardinal here, nor red, nor gray!No spies! Speak! Why are you afraid? The KingWants your opinion of the Cardinal.

DUKE DE BELLEGARDE.

Entirely frank, sire?

THE KING.

Yes, entirely frank.

DUKE DE BELLEGARDE (*boldly*).

Well, then, I think him a great man!

THE KING.

If needfulYou would proclaim it on the house-tops? Good!Can you not understand? The State, mark me,Is suffering, because he does it allAnd I am nothing!

DUKE DE BELLEGARDE.

Ah!

THE KING.

Rules he not warAnd peace, finances, states? Makes he not laws,Edicts, mandates, and ordinances too?Through treachery he broke the Catholic league;He strikes the house of Austria—friendlyTo me—to which the Queen belongs.

DUKE DE BELLEGARDE.

Ah, sire,He lets you keep a vivary withinThe Louvre. You have your share.

THE KING.

Then he intriguesWith Denmark.

DUKE DE BELLEGARDE.

But he let you fix the marcAmong the jewelers.

THE KING (*whose ill-humor increases*).

He fights with Rome!

DUKE DE BELLEGARDE.

He let you issue an edict, alone,By which a citizen was not allowedTo eat more than a crown's worth at a tavern,E'en though he wished to.

THE KING.

All the treaties heConcludes in secret.

DUKE DE BELLEGARDE.

Yes; but then you haveYour hunting mansion at Planchette.

THE KING.

All—all!He does it all! All with petitions rushTo him! I'm but a shadow to the French!Is there a single one who comes to meFor help?

DUKE DE BELLEGARDE.

Those who have the king's evil come.

[*The anger of* THE KING *increases.*

THE KING.
He means to give my order to his brother!I will not have it! I rebel.

DUKE DE BELLEGARDE.
But, sire—

THE KING.
I am disgusted with his people!

DUKE DE BELLEGARDE.
Sire!

THE KING.
His niece, Combalet, leads a model life.

DUKE DE BELLEGARDE.
'Tis slander, sire!

THE KING.
Two hundred foot-guards!

DUKE DE BELLEGARDE.
ButOnly a hundred horse-guards!

THE KING.
What a shame!

DUKE DE BELLEGARDE.
He saves France, sire.

THE KING.
Does he? He damns my soul!With one arm fights the heathen, with the otherHe signs a compact with the Huguenots.

[*Whispering to* DUKE DE BELLEGARDE.

Then, if I dared to count upon my handThe heads—the heads that fall for him at Grève!All friends of mine! His purple robes are madeOf their hearts' blood! 'Tis he who forces meTo wear eternal mourning.

DUKE DE BELLEGARDE.
Treats he his ownMore kindly? Did he spare Saint Preuil?

THE KING.
He hasA bitter tenderness, they say, for thoseHe loves. He must love me tremendously!

[*Abruptly, after a pause, folding his arms.*

He has exiled my mother!

DUKE DE BELLEGARDE.
But he thinksHe does your will. He's faithful. He is firmAnd sure.

THE KING.
I hate him! He is in my way.He crushes me! I am not master here—Not free! And yet I might be something. Ah,When he walks o'er me with such heavy tread,Does he not fear to rouse a slumbering king?For trembling near me, be it ne'er so high,His fortune vacillates with every breathI draw, and all would crumble at a word,Did I wish loud, what I wish in my heart!

[*A pause.*

That man makes good men bad, and bad men vile!The kingdom, like the king, already sick,Grows worse. Without is cardinal, withinIs cardinal; no king is anywhere!He torments Austria, lets any oneCapture my vessels in Gascony's Bay.Allies me with Gustavus Adolphus!What more? I do not know. He's everywhere:As if he were soul of the king, he fillsMy kingdom, and my family, and me.I am much to be pitied. [Going to window.Always rain.

DUKE DE BELLEGARDE.
Your Majesty is suffering?

THE KING.
I am bored.

[*A pause.*

39

I am the first in France and yet the last!I'd change my lot to lead a poacher's life—To hunt all day; to have no cares to fretThe pleasures of the chase; to sleep 'neath trees;To laugh at the King's officers, to singDuring the storm; to live as freely in the woodsAs birds live in the air. The peasant inHis hut, at least, is master and is king;But with that scarlet man forever there,Forever stern and cold, and speaking thus,"This must be your good pleasure, sire!" Oh, outrage!This man conceals me from my people's gaze.As with young children, he hides me beneathHis robe; and when a passer-by asks, "WhoIs that behind the Cardinal?" they say,"The King!" Then there are new lists every day.Last week the Huguenots; the duelistsTo-day! He wants their heads. Such a great crime—A duel! But the heads; what does he doWith them?

[DUKE DE BELLEGARDE *stamps his foot. Enter* MARQUIS DE NANGIS *and*MARION.

SCENE VII

The same. MARION, MARQUIS DE NANGIS. MARQUIS DE NANGIS *advances with his escort to within a few steps of* THE KING; *he kneels there.* MARION *falls on her knees at the door*

MARQUIS DE NANGIS.

Justice, my sire.

THE KING.

Against whom? Speak!

MARQUIS DE NANGIS.

Against a cruel tyrant—against Armand,Called here the cardinal-minister!

MARION.

Mercy,My sire!

THE KING.

For whom?

MARION.

For Didier!

MARQUIS DE NANGIS.

And for him,Gaspard de Saverny!

THE KING.

I've heard those names.

MARQUIS DE NANGIS.

Justice and mercy, sire!

THE KING.

What title?

MARQUIS DE NANGIS.

Sire,I am uncle of one.

THE KING.

And you?

MARION.

I'm sisterUnto the other!

THE KING.

Why do you come here,Sister and uncle?

MARQUIS DE NANGIS (*indicating first one of* THE KING'S *hands, then the other*).

To entreat mercyFrom this hand, and justice from that! My sire,I, William, Marquis de Nangis, CaptainOf Hundred Lances, Baron of MountainAnd Field, do make appeal to my two lords—The King of France and God, for justice 'gainstArmand du Plessis, Cardinal Richelieu.Gaspard de Saverny, for whom I makeThis prayer, is my nephew—

MARION (*low to* MARQUIS DE NANGIS).

Oh, speak for both,My lord!

MARQUIS DE NANGIS (*continuing*).

Last month he had a duel withA captain, a young nobleman, Didier.Of parentage uncertain. 'Twas a fault.They were too rash and brave. The ministerHad stationed sergeants—

THE KING.

Yes, I know the story.Well, what have you to say?

MARQUIS DE NANGIS.

That 'tis high timeYou thought about these things! The Cardinal-DukeHas more than one disastrous scheme afoot.He drinks the best blood of your subjects, sire!Your father, Henry IV., of royal heart,Would not have sacrificed his nobles thus!He never struck them down without dire need!Well served by them, he sought to guard them well.He knew good soldiers had more use in themThan trunkless heads. He knew their worth in war,This soldier-king whose doublet smelled of battle!Great days were those. I shared, I honor them!A few of the old race are living yet.Never could priest have touched one of those lords.There was no selling of a great head cheap!Sire, in these treacherous days to which we've come,Trust an old man, keep a few nobles dew.Perhaps, in your turn, you will need their help.The time may come when you will groan to thinkOf all the honors lavished on La Grève!Then, sadly, your regretful eyes will seekThose lords indomitably brave and true,Who, dead so long, had still been young to-day.The country's heart yet pants with civil war;The tocsin of past years re-echoes yet,Be saving of the executioner's arm!He is the one should sheathe his sword, not we!Be miserly with scaffolds, O my sire!'Twill be a woful thing some later dayTo mourn this great man's help, who hangs to-dayA whitening skeleton on gallows-tree!For blood, my king, is no good, wholesome dew.You'll reap no crops from irrigated Grève!The people will avoid the sight of kings.That flattering voice which tells you all is well,Tells you you're son of Henry IV., and Bourbon—That voice, my sire, however high it soars,Can never drown the thud of falling heads!Take my advice: play not this costly game.You, King, are bound to look God in the face,Hark to the words of fate, ere it rebels!War is a nobler thing than massacre!'Tis not a prosperous nor joyful StateWhen headsmen have more work than soldiers have!He for our country is a pastor hard,Who dares collect his tithes in slaughtered heads!Look! this proud lord of inhumanityWho holds your scepter has blood-covered hands!

THE KING.

The Cardinal's my friend! Who loves me mustLove him!

MARQUIS DE NANGIS.

Sire!

THE KING.

Silence! He's my second self.

MARQUIS DE NANGIS.

Sire!

THE KING.

Bring no more such griefs to trouble me!

[*Showing his hair, which is beginning to turn gray.*

Petitioners like you make these gray hairs!

MARQUIS DE NANGIS.

An old man, sire; a woman, sire, who weeps!A word from you is life or death for us!

THE KING.

What do you ask?

MARQUIS DE NANGIS.

Pardon for my Gaspard!

MARION.

Pardon for Didier!

THE KING.

Pardons of a kingAre often thefts from justice!

MARION.

Oh, no, sire!Since God himself is merciful, you needNot fear! Have pity! Two young, thoughtless men,Pushed by this duel o'er a precipiceTo die! Good God! to die upon the gallows!You will have pity, won't you? I don't knowHow people talk to kings—I'm but a woman;To weep so much perhaps is wrong. But oh,A monster is that cardinal of yours.Why does he hate them? They did naught to him.He never saw my Didier. All who doMust love him! They're so young—these two! To dieFor just a duel! Think about their mothers.Oh, it is horrible! You will not do it, sire!We women cannot talk as well as men.We've only cries and tears and knees, which bendAnd totter as kings turn their eyes on us.They were in fault, of course! But if they brokeYour law, you can forgive it! What is youth?Young people are so

41

heedless! For a look,A word, a trifle, anything or nothing,They always lose their heads like that! Such thingsAre happening every day. Each noble, here,He knows it. Ask them, sire! Is it not true,My lords? Oh, frightful hour of agony!To know with one word you can save two lives!I'd love you all my life, sire, if you wouldHave mercy—mercy, God! If I knew how,I'd talk so that you'd have to say that word.You'd pardon them; you'd say, "I must consoleThat woman, for her Didier is her soul."I suffocate, sire. Pity, pity me!

THE KING.

Who is this woman?

MARION.

She's a sister, sire,Who trembles at your feet. You owe somethingUnto your people!

THE KING.

Yes! I owe myselfTo them, and dueling does grievous harm.

MARION.

You should have pity!

THE KING.

And obedience, too!

MARQUIS DE NANGIS.

Two boys of twenty years! Think of it well!Their years together are but half of mine!

MARION.

Your Majesty, you have a mother, wife,A son—some one at least who's dear to you!A brother? Then have pity for a sister!

THE KING.

No, I have not a brother! [*Reflects a moment.*Yes, *Monsieur!*

[*Perceiving the escort of* MARQUIS DE NANGIS.

Well, my lord marquis, what is this brigade?Are we besieged, or off to the Crusades?To bring your guards thus boldly in my sight,Are you a duke and peer?

MARQUIS DE NANGIS.

I'm better, sire,Than any duke and peer, created for mere show!I'm Breton baron of four baronies.

DUKE DE BELLEGARDE (*aside*).

His pride is great, and here, unfortunate!

THE KING.

Good! To your manors carry back your rights,And leave us ours within our own domain.We are justiciary!

MARQUIS DE NANGIS (*shuddering*).

Sire, reflect!Think of their age, their expiated fault!

[*Falling on his knees.*

The pride of an old man, who, prostrate, kneels!Have mercy!

[THE KING *makes an abrupt sign of anger and refusal.*

I was comrade to Henry!Your father and our father! I was thereWhen he—that monster—struck the fatal blow.'Til night I watched beside my royal dead:It was my duty. I have seen my fatherAnd my six brothers fall 'neath rival factions;I have lost the wife who loved me. NowThe old man standing here is like a victimWhom a hard executioner, for sport,Has bound unto the wheel the whole long day.My master, God has broken every limbWith His great iron rod! 'Tis night-time now,And I've received the final blow! Farewell,My king! God keep you!

[*He makes a profound obeisance, and exits.* MARION *lifts herself with difficulty, and, staggering, falls on the threshold of the gilt door of* THE KING'S *private room.*

THE KING (*to* DUKE DE BELLEGARDE, *wiping his eyes and watching the retreating figure of* MARQUIS DE NANGIS).

A sad interview!Ah, not to weaken, kings must watch themselves!To do right is not easy. I was touched.

[*Reflects for a moment, then interrupts himself suddenly.*

No pardoning to-day, for yesterdayI sinned too much!

[*Approaching* DUKE DE BELLEGARDE.

Before he came, my lord,You said bold things, which may be bad for youWhen I report to my lord cardinalThe conversation we have had. I'm sorryFor you, Duke. In the future, have more care!I slept so wretchedly, my poor Bellegarde.

[*With a gesture dismissing Courtiers and Guards.*

Pray leave us, gentlemen![*To* L'ANGELY.] Stay, you!

[*All go out except* MARION, *whom* THE KING *does not see.* DUKE DE BELLEGARDE *sees her crouching on the threshold of the door and goes to her.*

DUKE DE BELLEGARDE (*low to* MARION).

My child,You can't remain here, crouching by this door;What are you doing like a statue there?Get up and go away!

MARION.

I'm waiting hereFor them to kill me!

L'ANGELY (*low to* DUKE DE BELLEGARDE).

Leave her there, my lord![*Low to* MARION.] Remain!

[*He returns to* THE KING, *who is seated in the great armchair and is in a profound reverie.*

SCENE VIII

THE KING, L'ANGELY

THE KING (*sighing deeply*).

Ah! L'Angely, my heart is sick.'Tis full of bitterness. I cannot smile.You, only, have the power to cheer me. Come!You stand in no awe of my majesty.Come, throw a glint of pleasure in my soul.

[*A pause.*

L'ANGELY.

Life is a bitter thing, your Majesty.

THE KING.

Alas!

L'ANGELY.

Man is a breath ephemeral!

THE KING.

A breath, and nothing more!

L'ANGELY.

UnfortunateIs any one who is both man and king.Is it not true?

THE KING.

A double burden—yes.

L'ANGELY.

And better far than life, sire, is the tomb,If but its gloom is deep enough!

THE KING.

I've thoughtThat always!

L'ANGELY.

To be dead or unborn isThe only happiness. Yes, man's condemned!

THE KING.

You give me pleasure when you talk like this!

[*A silence.*

L'ANGELY.

Once in the tomb, think you one e'er gets out?

THE KING (*whose sadness has increased with the Fool's words*).

We'll know that later. I wish I were there!

[*Silence.*

Fool, I'm unhappy! Do you comprehend?

L'ANGELY.

I see it in your face so thin and worn,And in your mourning—

THE KING.

Ah, why should I laugh?Your tricks are lost on me! What use is lifeTo you? The fine profession! Jester to the King!Bell out of tune, a jumping-jack to play with,Whose half-cracked laugh is but a poor grimace!What is there in the world for you, poor toy?Why do you live?

43

L'ANGELY.

For curiosity.But you—why should you live? I pity you!I'd sooner be a woman than a kingLike you. I'm but a jumping-jack whose stringYou hold; but underneath your royal coatThere's hid a tauter string, a strong arm holds.Better a jumping-jack in a king's handsThan in a priest's, my sire.

[*Silence.*

THE KING (*thinking, growing more and more sad*).

You speak the truth,Although you laugh. He is a fearful man!Has Satan made himself a cardinal?What if 'twere Satan who possessed my soul!What say you?

L'ANGELY.

I have often had that thoughtMyself!

THE KING.

We must not speak thus. 'Tis a sin!Behold, how dire misfortune follows me!I had some Spanish cormorants. I comeTo this place—not a drop of water hereFor fishing! In the country! Not a pondIn this accursed Chambord large enoughTo drown a flesh-worm! When I wish to hunt—The sea! And when I wish to fish—the fields!Am I unfortunate enough?

L'ANGELY.

Your lifeIs full of woe.

THE KING.

How will you comfort me?

L'ANGELY.

Another grief! You hold in high esteem,And justly too, the art of training hawksFor hunting partridges. A good huntsman—You're one—ought to respect the falconer.

THE KING.

The falconer! A god!

L'ANGELY.

Well! there are twoWho are at point of death!

THE KING.

Two falconers?

L'ANGELY.

Yes!

THE KING.

Who are they?

L'ANGELY.

Two famous ones!

THE KING.

But who?

L'ANGELY.

Those two young men whose lives were begged of you!

THE KING.

Gaspard and Didier?

L'ANGELY.

Yes; they are the last.

THE KING.

What a calamity! Two falconers!Now that the art is very nearly lost.Unhappy duel! When I'm dead, this artWill go from earth, as all things go at last!Why did they fight this duel?

L'ANGELY.

One declaredThat hawks upon the wing were not as swiftAs falcons.

THE KING.

He was wrong. But yet that seemsScarcely a hanging matter— [*Silence.*And my rightOf pardon is inviolable—thoughI am too lenient, says the Cardinal! [*Silence.*[*To* L'ANGELY.] The Cardinal desires their death?

L'ANGELY.

He does!

THE KING (*after pausing and reflecting*).

44

Then they shall die!

L'ANGELY.

They shall!

THE KING.

Poor falconry!

L'ANGELY (*going to window*).

Sire, look!

THE KING (*turns around suddenly*).

At what?

L'ANGELY.

Just look, I beg of you!

THE KING (*rising and going to the window*).

What is it?

L'ANGELY (*indicating something outside*).

They have changed the sentinel!

THE KING.

Well, is that all?

L'ANGELY.

Who is that fellow withThe yellow lace?

THE KING.

No one—the corporal!

L'ANGELY.

He puts a new man there. What says he, low?

THE KING.

The password! Fool! What are you driving at?

L'ANGELY.

At this: Kings act the part of sentinels.Instead of pikes, a scepter they must bear.When they have strutted 'round their little day,Death comes—the corporal of kings—and putsAnother scepter-bearer in their place,Speaking the password which God sends, and whichIs clemency.

THE KING.

No, it is justice. Ah,Two falconers! It is a frightful loss!Still, they must die.

L'ANGELY.

As you must die, and I.Or big or little, death has appetiteFor all. But though they've not much room,The dead sleep well. The Cardinal annoysAnd wearies you. Wait, sire! A day, a month,A year; when we have played as long as needful—I, my own part of fool; you, king; and he,The master—we will go to sleep. No matterHow proud or great we are, no one shall haveMore than six feet of territory there.Look! how they bear his lordly litter now!

THE KING.

Yes, life is dark; the tomb alone is bright.If you were not at hand to cheer me up—

L'ANGELY.

Alas! I came to-day to say farewell.

THE KING.

What's that?

L'ANGELY.

I leave you!

THE KING.

You're a crazy fool!Death, only, frees from royal service.

L'ANGELY.

Well,I am about to die!

THE KING.

Have you gone mad?

L'ANGELY.

You have condemned me—you, the King of France!

THE KING.

If you are joking, fool, explain yourself.

L'ANGELY.

I shared the duel of those two young men—At least my sword did, sire, if I did not.I here surrender it.

[Draws his sword and, kneeling, presents it to THE KING.

THE KING *(takes it and examines it).*

Indeed, a sword!Where does it come from, friend?

L'ANGELY.

We're noble, sire!The guilty are not pardoned. I am one.

THE KING *(somber and stern).*

Good night, then! Let me kiss your neck, poor fool,Before they cut it off.

[Embraces L'ANGELY.

L'ANGELY *(aside).*

He's in dead earnest!

THE KING *(after a pause).*

For never does a worthy king opposeThe course of justice. But you claim too much,Lord Cardinal—two falconers and my fool!All for one duel!

[Greatly agitated, he walks up and down with his hand on his forehead. Then he turns to L'ANGELY, *who is most anxious.*

Go! console yourself!Life is but bitterness, the tomb means rest.Man is a breath ephemeral.

L'ANGELY *(aside).*

The devil!

*[*THE KING *continues to pace the floor and appears violently agitated.*

THE KING.

And so, you think you'll have to hang, poor fool!

L'ANGELY *(aside).*

He means it! God! I feel cold perspirationStarting upon my brow.*[Aloud.]* Unless a wordFrom you—

THE KING.

Whom shall I have to make me laugh?If you should rise from out the tomb, come backAnd tell me all about it. 'Tis a chance!

L'ANGELY.

The errand is a pleasant one!

*[*THE KING *continues to walk rapidly, speaking to* L'ANGELY *now and then.*

THE KING.

What triumphFor my lord cardinal—my fool!

[Folding his arms.

Think youI could be master if I wished to be?

L'ANGELY.

Montaigne would say, "Who knows?" And Rabelais,"Perhaps."

THE KING *(with gesture of determination).*

Give me a parchment, fool.

*[*L'ANGELY *eagerly hands a parchment which he finds on the table near the writing-desk.* THE KING *hastily writes a few words, then gives the parchment back to* L'ANGELY.

Behold!I pardon all.

L'ANGELY.

All three?

THE KING.

Yes.

L'ANGELY *(running to* MARION).

Come, madame,Come, kneel, and thank the King.

MARION *(falling on her knees).*

We have the pardon?

L'ANGELY.

Yes! It was I—

MARION.

Whose knees must I embrace—His Majesty's or yours?
THE KING (*astonished, examining* MARION: *aside*).
What does this mean?Is this a trap?
L'ANGELY (*giving parchment to* MARION).
Here is the pardon. Take it!
[MARION *kisses it, and puts it in her bosom.*
THE KING (*aside*).
Have I been duped?[*To* MARION.] One instant! Give it back!
MARION.
Good God!
[*To* THE KING, *with courage, touching her breast.*
Come here and take it, and tear outMy heart as well!
[THE KING *stops and steps backward, much embarrassed.*
L'ANGELY (*low to* MARION).
Good! Keep it, and be firm!His Majesty won't take it, there!
THE KING (*to* MARION).
Give itTo me!
MARION.
Take it, my sire!
THE KING (*casting down his eyes*).
Who is this siren?
L'ANGELY (*low to* MARION).
He wouldn't touch the corset of the Queen!
THE KING (*after a moment's hesitation, dismisses* MARION *with a gesture without looking at her*).
Well, go!
MARION (*bowing profoundly to* THE KING).
I'll fly to save the prisoners! [*Exits.*
L'ANGELY (*to* THE KING).
She's sister to Didier, the falconer.
THE KING.
She can be what she will. It's very strange,The way she made me drop my eyes! Made me,A man— [*Silence.*Fool, you have played a trick on me!I'll have to pardon you a second time.
L'ANGELY.
Yes, do it! Every time they grant a pardon,Kings lift a dreary weight from off their hearts.
THE KING.
You speak the truth. I always suffer whenLa Grève holds court. Nangis was right: the deadServe nobody. To fill MontfauconI make a desert of the Louvre!
[*Walking rapidly.*
'Tis treasonTo strike my right of pardon out, beforeMy face. What can I do?
Disarmed, dethroned,And fallen: in this man absorbed, as inA sepulcher! His cloak becomes my shroud:My people mourn for me as for the dead.I am resolved: those two boys shall not die!The joy of living is a heavenly gift.
[*After reflection.*
God, who knows where we go, can ope the tomb;A king cannot. Back to their familiesI give them; that old man, that fair young girl,Will bless me. It is said: I've signed it—I,The King. The Cardinal will be furious,But it will please Bellegarde.
L'ANGELY.
One can, sometimes,Be kingly by mistake.

ACT V

THE CARDINAL

SCENE.—*Beaugency. The tower of Beaugency. A courtyard; the tower in the background, all around a high wall. To the left, a tall arched door; to the right, a small rounded door in the wall; near the door a stone table and stone bench*

47

SCENE I

Some Workmen. They are pulling down a corner of the back wall on the left. The demolition is almost completed

FIRST WORKMAN (*working with his pickax*).

It's very hard!

SECOND WORKMAN (*working*).

Deuce take this heavy wall we're pulling down!

THIRD WORKMAN (*working*).

Saw you the scaffold, Peter?

FIRST WORKMAN.

Yes, I did.

[*He goes to the large door and measures it.*

The door is narrow; never will the litterOf the Lord Cardinal go through it.

THIRD WORKMAN.

Bah!Is it a house?

FIRST WORKMAN (*with affirmative gesture*).

With great long curtains. Yes.It takes some four and twenty men on footTo carry it.

SECOND WORKMAN.

I saw the great machine,One night when it was very dark. It lookedJust like Leviathan in shadow-land.

THIRD WORKMAN.

What does he come here with his sergeants for?

FIRST WORKMAN.

To see the execution of those two young men.He's sick. He needs to be amused.

SECOND WORKMAN.

To work!

[*They resume work; the wall is about torn down.*

Saw you the scaffold, all in black? That comesOf being noble!

FIRST WORKMAN.

They have everything.

SECOND WORKMAN.

I wonderIf they would build a black scaffold for us.

FIRST WORKMAN.

What have those young men done that they should die?Hein? Do you understand, Maurice?

THIRD WORKMAN.

I don't.It's justice.

[*They continue their work.* LAFFEMAS *enters;* THE WORKMEN *are silent. He comes from the back as though he were coming from an inside court of the prison; stops beside* THE WORKMEN, *appears to examine the breach, and gives them some directions. When the space is opened, he orders them to hang black cloth across it, which covers it entirely; then he dismisses them. At almost the same moment* MARION*appears, dressed in white, and veiled; she enters through the great door, crosses the court rapidly, and runs to the grating of the small door, at which she knocks.* LAFFEMAS *follows slowly in the same direction. The grating is opened;* THE TURNKEY *appears.*

SCENE II

MARION, LAFFEMAS

MARION (*showing a parchment to* THE TURNKEY).

Order of the King!

THE TURNKEY.

You can'tEnter, madame.

MARION.

What!

LAFFEMAS (*presenting a paper to* THE TURNKEY).

Signed, the Cardinal!

THE TURNKEY.

Enter.

48

[*When about to enter,* LAFFEMAS *turns, looks at* MARION *a moment, then approaches her.* THE
TURNKEY *shuts the door.*

LAFFEMAS (*to* MARION).
You here? This questionable place!

MARION.
I am. [*Triumphantly showing the parchment.*I have the pardon!

LAFFEMAS (*showing his*).
Yes? I haveThe revocation!

MARION (*with a cry of horror*).
Mine was yesterday—The morning!

LAFFEMAS.
Mine, last night!

MARION (*with hands over her eyes*).
My God! No hope!

LAFFEMAS.
Hope is a flash of lightning which deceives.The clemency of kings is a frail thing;It
comes with lagging steps and goes with wings.

MARION.
The King was moved with pity for their fate!

LAFFEMAS.
What can the King against the Cardinal?

MARION.
Oh, Didier, our last hope's extinguished now!

LAFFEMAS (*low*).
Not—not the last!

MARION.
Just Heaven!

LAFFEMAS (*drawing near to her*).
There is hereA man whom one short word from you could makeHappier than any
king, and mightier too!

MARION.
Away!

LAFFEMAS.
Is that your answer?

MARION (*haughtily*).
I beg you!

LAFFEMAS.
How fleeting are the whims of the fair sex!You were not always, madame, so
severe!Now that 'tis question of your lover's life—

MARION (*without looking at him, turning to the small door, her hands clasped*).
If it would save your life, I could not goBack to that infamy. My soul's grown pureAt
touch of you, my Didier; sin is shamed.Your love gives back my lost virginity.

LAFFEMAS.
Well, love him!

MARION.
Ah, he pushes me from crimeTo vice! Oh, monster, go! Let me keep pure!

LAFFEMAS.
There is but one thing left for me to do!

MARION.
What is it?

LAFFEMAS.
I can show you—let you see.It is to-night.

MARION (*trembling all over*).
Oh, heaven! this night!

LAFFEMAS.
This nightThe Cardinal, in litter, will attend.

[MARION *is buried in a deep and painful reverie. Suddenly she passes her two hands over her brow and turns, as if wild, toward* LAFFEMAS.

MARION.

How could you manage their escape?

LAFFEMAS (*low*).

You mean?Two of my men could guard this place, by whichThe Cardinal passes—

[*He listens at the small door.*

I think some one comes!

MARION (*wringing her hands*).

You'll save him?

LAFFEMAS.

Yes.[*Low.*] To tell you in this place—The walls have echoes—elsewhere.

MARION (*with despair*).

Come!

[LAFFEMAS *goes toward the large door and signs to her to follow. She falls on her knees, turned toward the grating of the prison; then she arises with a convulsive effort and disappears through the great door after* LAFFEMAS. SAVERNY *and* DIDIER *enter, surrounded by Guards.*

SCENE III

DIDIER, SAVERNY. SAVERNY, *dressed in the latest fashion, enters gayly and petulantly.* DIDIER *is in black, walks slowly, is very pale. A jailer accompanied by Halberdiers conducts them.* THE JAILER *places the two Halberdiers as sentinels beside the black curtain.* DIDIER *sits, silently, on the stone bench*

SAVERNY (*to* THE JAILER, *who opens the door for him*).

Thank you.The air is very good!

THE JAILER (*low, and drawing him aside*).

My lord, two words with you.

SAVERNY.

Four, if you like.

THE JAILER (*lowering his voice still more*).

Will you escape?

SAVERNY (*eagerly*).

Speak! How?

THE JAILER.

That's my affair.

SAVERNY.

Truly? [THE JAILER *nods his head.*Lord Cardinal,You meant to keep me from attending balls,But it appears I am to dance again.The pleasant thing that life is![*To* THE JAILER.] When, my friend?

THE JAILER.

To-night, as soon as it is dark.

SAVERNY.

My faith!I shall be charmed to leave these quarters. WhenceComes this assistance?

THE JAILER.

Marquis de Nangis.

SAVERNY.

My good old uncle![*To* THE JAILER.] 'Tis for both, I hope!

THE JAILER.

I can save only one!

SAVERNY.

For twice as much?

THE JAILER.

I can save only one!

SAVERNY (*tossing his head*).

Just one?[*Low to* THE JAILER.] Then listen;Good jailer, that's the one to save!

[*Indicating* DIDIER.

THE JAILER.

You jest!
SAVERNY.
I do not! He's the one!
THE JAILER.
What an idea!Your uncle wants to save you, not save him.
SAVERNY.
It's settled? Then prepare two shrouds at once.
[*Turns his back on* THE JAILER, *who goes out, astonished.* A REGISTRAR*enters.*
We can't be left alone an instant—strange!
REGISTRAR (*saluting the prisoners*).
The royal councilor of the Great ChamberIs close at hand.
[*Salutes them again and exits.*
SAVERNY.
'Tis well! [*Laughing.*Annoying luck!Twenty years old—September—and to dieBefore October!
DIDIER (*motionless at front of stage, holding the portrait in his hand, and as if absorbed in a deep study of it*).
Come, look at me well!Eyes in my eyes: thus. You are beautiful!What radiant grace! Hardly a woman, you!No: much more like an angel. God HimselfWhen He formed that divinely honest lookPut much fire in it but more chastity.That childish mouth, pushed open by sweet hopes,Throbs with its innocence.
[*Throwing the portrait violently to the ground.*
Why did that peasantTake me unto her breast? Why not have dashedMy head against the stones? What did I doUnto my mother to be cursed with birth?Why, in that misery, it may be crime,Which forced her to abandon her own blood,Had she not motherhood enough to chokeMe in her arms?
SAVERNY (*returning from back of court*).
The swallows fly quite low;'Twill rain to-night.
DIDIER (*without hearing him*).
A faithless, a mad thing,A woman is: inconstant, cruel, deep,And turbulent as is the ocean. Ah,Upon that sea I trusted all my fortune!In all the vast horizon saw one star!Well! I am shipwrecked! Nothing's left but death.Yet I was born good-hearted: might have foundThe spark divine within me by-and-by.Fair looked the future! Oh, remorseless woman,Did you not shrink in face of such a lie,Since to your mercy I trusted my soul?
SAVERNY.
Forever Marion! You've strange ideasAbout her!
DIDIER (*without heeding him, picks up the picture and fixes his eyes upon it*).
Down 'mongst the degraded thingsI must throw you, oh, woman who betrays!A demon, with eyes touched by angels' wings.
[*Puts it back into his breast.*
Come back; here is your place![*Approaching* SAVERNY.] A curious thing!That portrait is alive; I do not jest.While you were sleeping there so peacefullyIt gnawed my heart all night.
SAVERNY.
Alas! poor friend.We'll talk of death.[*Aside.*] It comforts him, althoughI find it rather sad.
DIDIER.
What did you say?I have not listened. Since I heard that nameI have been stupefied. I cannot think:I can't remember, cannot hear nor see!
SAVERNY (*taking hold of his arm*).
Death, friend!
DIDIER (*joyfully*).
Oh, yes!
SAVERNY.
Let's talk about it.
DIDIER.
Yes!

SAVERNY.
What is it, after all?
DIDIER.
Did you sleep wellLast night?
SAVERNY.
No, badly, for my bed was hard.
DIDIER.
When you are dead, your bed will be much harder,But you will sleep extremely well—that's all.They've made hell splendidly; but by the sideOf life, it's nothing.
SAVERNY.
Good! My fears are gone!But to be hanged! That certainly is bad.
DIDIER.
You're getting death; don't be an egotist.
SAVERNY.
You can be satisfied; but I am not.I'm not afraid of death—that is no boast—When death is death, but on the gallows!
DIDIER.
Well,Death has a thousand forms—gallows are one.That moment is not pleasant when the ropePuts out your life as one puts out a flame,Choking your throat to let your soul fly up;But, after all, what matter? If all's dark,If only all this earth is hidden well,What matter if a tomb lies on one's breast?What matter if the night-winds howl and blowAbout the strings of flesh crows tore from youWhen you were on the gibbet? What care you?
SAVERNY.
You're a philosopher.
DIDIER.
Yes, let them rave.Let vultures tear my flesh, let worms consume,As they consume all, even kings; my bodyIs what's concerned, not I. What do I care?When sepulchers shut down our mortal eye,The soul lifts up the mighty mass of stoneAnd flies away—
[A Councilor enters, preceded and followed by Halberdiers in black.
SCENE IV
The same. COUNCILOR OF THE GREAT CHAMBER, in full dress, THE JAILER, Guards
THE JAILER (announcing).
The Councilor of the King!
COUNCILOR (saluting SAVERNY and DIDIER in turn).
My mission's painful and the law severe—
SAVERNY.
I understand: there is no hope! Speak, sir!
COUNCILOR (unfolds a parchment and reads).
"We, Louis, King of France and of Navarre,Reject appeals made by these men condemned,But moved by pity, change the punishmentAnd order them beheaded."
SAVERNY (joyfully).
God be praised!
COUNCILOR (saluting them once more).
You are to hold yourselves in readiness;It will take place to-day.
[He salutes and prepares to exit.
DIDIER (who has remained in the same thoughtful attitude, to SAVERNY).
As I was saying,After this death, although the corpse be mangled,Though every limb be stamped with hideous wounds,Though arms be twisted, broken every bone,Though through the mire the body has been dragged,From out that putrid, bleeding, awful fleshThe soul shall rise, unstained, untouched, and pure.
COUNCILOR (coming back, to DIDIER).
'Tis well to occupy yourselves with suchGreat thoughts.
DIDIER (gently).
Please do not interrupt me, sir.
SAVERNY (gayly to DIDIER).
No gallows!

DIDIER.

Order of the fête is changed,I know. The Cardinal travels with his headsman,And he must be employed; the ax will rust.

SAVERNY.

You're cool about it, yet the stake is great.[*To* THE COUNCILOR.] Thank you for such good news.

COUNCILOR.

I wish 'twere better!Good sir, my zeal—

SAVERNY.

Excuse me. What's the hour?

COUNCILOR.

At nine o'clock to-night.

DIDIER.

I hope the skyWill be as dark as is my soul.

SAVERNY.

The place?

COUNCILOR (*indicating the neighboring court*).

Here in the court. The Cardinal will come.

[COUNCILOR *exits with his escort. The two prisoners remain alone. Day begins to fade. The halberds of the two sentinels, who silently promenade before the breach, are all that can be seen.*

DIDIER (*solemnly, after a pause*).

At this portentous hour we must reflectUpon the fate awaiting us. Our yearsAre equal, though I'm older far than you.It is but just, therefore, that mine should beThe voice to cheer and to exhort you, sinceI am the cause of all your misery.'Twas I who challenged you. You were contentAnd happy: 'twas enough for me to passAcross your life to ruin it. My fatePressed down upon yours 'til it crushed it. Now,Together, we are soon to face the tomb.We'll take each other's hand—

[*Sound of hammering.*

SAVERNY.

What is that noise?

DIDIER.

It is our scaffold which they're building, orOur coffins they are nailing.

[SAVERNY *sits on the stone bench.*

When the hourHas tolled, sometimes the heart of man gives way.Life holds us in a thousand secret ways.

[*A bell strikes.*

I think a voice is calling to us. Hark!

[*Another bell.*

SAVERNY.

The hour is striking.

[*A third bell.*

DIDIER.

Yes, the hour!

[*A fourth bell.*

SAVERNY.

In chapel!

[*Four more bells.*

DIDIER.

It is a voice that calls us, just the same.

SAVERNY.

Another hour!

[*He leans his elbows on the stone table and drops his head on his hands. The Guard is changed.*

DIDIER.

My friend, do not give way!Don't falter on this threshold we must cross.The tomb they're fitting up for us is low,And won't permit the entrance of a head.Let's go to meet them with a fearless tread.The scaffold can afford to shake, not we.They claim our heads; and since no fault is ours,We'll bear them proudly to the fatal block.

[*Approaches* SAVERNY, *who is motionless.*

Courage!

[*Touches his arm and finds he is asleep.*

Asleep! While I've been preaching courageThis man has slept! What is my braveryCompared to his? Sleep on, you who can sleep.My turn will come—provided all things die,That nothing of the heart survives withinThe tomb, to hate what it has loved too much.

[*It is night. While* DIDIER *has become absorbed in his thoughts,*MARION *and* THE JAILER *enter through the opening in the wall;* THE JAILER *precedes her. He carries a dark-lantern and a bundle, both of which he places on the ground, then advances cautiously toward*MARION, *who has remained standing on the threshold, pale, motionless, half-wild.*

SCENE VI

[The scenes are mis-numbered in the book and skip from the number IV to the number VI in Act V. (note of etext transcriber)]

The same. MARION, THE JAILER

THE JAILER (*to* MARION.)

Be sure to come at the appointed hour.

[*Goes up stage; during the rest of this scene he continues to walk up and down at the back.*

MARION (*advances with tottering steps as if absorbed in some desperate thought. Every now and then she draws her hand across her face as if to rub off something*).

His lips, like red-hot iron, have branded me!

[*Suddenly she discovers* DIDIER, *gives a cry, runs and throws herself breathless at his feet.*

Didier—Didier!

DIDIER (*roused with a start*).

Here, Marion! My God![*Coldly.*] 'Tis you?

MARION.

Who should it be? Oh, leave me here—Here at your feet! It is the place I love!Your hands, your dear loved hands, give them—your hands!Oh, they are wounded! Those harsh chains did that.The wretched creatures! But I'm here—you know—Oh, it is terrible! [*She weeps; her sobs are audible.*

DIDIER.

Why do you weep?

MARION.

Why? Didier, I'm not weeping! No, I laugh!

[*She laughs.*

We'll soon escape from here! I laugh. I'm happy.You will live; the danger's passed.

[*She falls again at* DIDIER'S *feet and sobs.*

My God!All this is killing me! I'm broken—crushed.

DIDIER.

Madame—

MARION (*rises, without hearing him, and gets the bundle and brings it to him*).

Now hurry! We have not much time!Take this disguise. I've bribed the sentinels.We'll leave Beaugency without being seen.Go down that street, at the wall's end, out there!The Cardinal will come to see them executeHis orders; we can't lose an instant now.The cannon will be fired when he arrives,And we'll be lost if we should still be here.

DIDIER.

'Tis well!

MARION.

Quick! hurry! Didier, you are saved!To be free! Didier, how I love you—God!

DIDIER.

You say a street where the wall ends?

MARION.

I do.I saw it. I've been there. It is quite safe.I saw them close up the last window, too.It may be we shall meet some women, butThey'll think you're just a passer-by. Come, love;When you are far off—please put on these things—We'll laugh to see you thus disguised. Come, dear!

DIDIER (*pushing the clothes aside with his foot*).

There is no hurry.

MARION.

Death waits at the door.Fly! Didier! Since I've come!

DIDIER.

Why did you come?

MARION.

To save you! What a question to ask me!Why such a freezing tone?

DIDIER (*with a sad smile*).

Ah, well! We menAre often senseless.

MARION.

We are losing time.The horses wait. What you have in your mind,You'll tell me afterward. We must fly now.

DIDIER.

Who is that man there watching us?

MARION.

The jailer.He's safe; I bribed him, as I did the guard.Do you suspect them? You have such an air.

DIDIER.

It's nothing. We're so easily deceived.

MARION.

Come! Each lost moment chills me to the heart.I seem to hear the tread of that great crowd.Hasten, my Didier—on my knees—oh, fly!

DIDIER (*indicating* SAVERNY, *asleep*).

Tell me which one of us you want to save.

MARION (*overcome for a moment*).

[*Aside.*] Gaspard is generous: he would not tell.[*Aloud.*] Does Didier speak to his beloved thus?My Didier, what have you against me?

DIDIER.

Naught.Lift up your face and look me in the eyes.

[MARION, *trembling, fixes her eyes on him.*

It is a perfect likeness! Yes.

MARION.

My love,I worship you, but come!

DIDIER.

Don't turn away!

[*He looks at her fixedly.*

MARION (*terrified at his look*).

[*Aside.*] The kisses of that man, he sees them! God![*Aloud.*] You have a secret, something against me!It hurts you! Tell me all about it, dear.You know we often make things worse by thinking,And too late find it out; then we regret.I had my share in all your thoughts, love, once!Speak, are those days for evermore gone by?Do you not love me now? Have you forgotMy little room at Blois? Forgotten howWe loved each other, till the world was lost?Sometimes you grew uneasy; then I said,"If any one should see him!" Oh, 'twas fine!But one day has destroyed it all. You've saidA thousand times, in words that burned my soul,I was your love, I knew your secrets, ICould make you anything I chose. What haveI ever asked? I've always thought with you!This time, oh, yield to me! It is your lifeI'm pleading for. My Didier, hark to me.Alive or dead, I swear to follow you.All things with you, love, will be sweet to me—To fly, or die upon the scaffold. What!You push me back? You shall not! Leave your hand,I want it. My poor brow, it does no harmTo rest it on your knees. I am so tired;I ran so fast to come! What would they say,The people I knew once, to see me now?I was so gay, so merry; now I weep!What is it that you have against me? Speak!Oh, shame! You must let me lie at your feet.It's very cruel of you not to sayOne single word. When we have thoughts, we speak!'Twould be more merciful to stab me, love!See, I have

dried my tears, and I am smiling.You smile too. Oh, if you don't smile at me,I will not love
you! I have always doneJust what you wanted; now it is your turn.These chains are what have
chilled your soul. Love, smileAnd speak to me, and say "Marie."
DIDIER.
"Marie"Or "Marion"?
MARION (*falls annihilated at his feet*).
Didier, be merciful!
DIDIER (*with terrible tone*).
Here, no one finds an entrance easily.Prisons of state are guarded night and day,The
doors are iron, walls twenty cubits high;To open these remorseless doors, madame,To whom
here did you prostitute yourself?
MARION.
Who told you?
DIDIER.
No one; but I understand.
MARION.
Didier, I swear by every hope divineIt was to save you, tear you from this place;To
melt the executioner—to save you—Don't you hear?
DIDIER (*folding his arms*).
I thank you! To descendAs low as that! To have no shame, no soul!Oh, madame! can
one be so infamous?
[*Crossing the court with a great cry of rage.*
Who is this trader in disgrace and vice,Who puts a price like that upon my
head?Where is the jailer, where the judge, the man?—That I may crush him as I crush this
thing.
[*He is about to break the portrait in his hands, but he stops, and beside himself, continues.*
The judge? Yes, gentlemen, make laws and judge!What matters it to me if the false
weightWhich swings your vile scales to this side or thatBe made of woman's honor or man's
life?[*To* MARION.] Go to your lover!
MARION.
Do not treat me thus!Another word of scorn and I fall deadHere at your feet. If ever
love was trueAnd strong and pure, mine was. If any manWas ever worshiped by a woman,
youHave been by me.
DIDIER.
Hush! Do not speak! I might,For sorrow, have been born a woman too.I might have
been as infamous as you.I might have sold myself, have given my breastTo any passer-by, as
place for rest.But if there came to me, in his frank way,An honest man, filled with the love of
truth,If I had met a heart insane enoughTo keep its vain illusions all these years,Oh, sooner
than not tell that honest man"I'm this," sooner than charm and dazzle him,Sooner than fail
to warn him that my eyesSo candid and my lips so pure were lies,Sooner than be perfidious
and base like that,I'd want to dig my grave with my own hands.
MARION.
O God!
DIDIER.
How you would laugh if you could seeThe picture that my heart painted of you!How
wise you were to shatter it, madame!There you were chaste and beautiful and pure!What
injury has this poor man done you,Who loved you on his bended knees?
[*Presenting portrait to her.*
PerhapsThis is a fitting time to give you backThis pledge of love ardent and true.
MARION (*turning away with a cry*).
Oh, shame!
DIDIER.
Did you not have it painted just for me?
[*He laughs, and dashes the locket to the ground.*
MARION.
Will some one, out of pity, kill me now?

THE JAILER.
Time's passing.
MARION.
Yes, it flies; and we are lost.Didier, I've not the right to say a single word.I am a woman to whom naught is due.You have rebuked and cursed me: you did well!I merit still more hate and shame. You've beenToo kind; my broken, bruised heart is grateful.But the remorseless hour draws near. Away!The headsman you forget, remembers you.I've planned it all. You can escape. Now, listen—My God! do not refuse. You know how muchIt costs me. Hate me, strike me, curse me, leaveMe to my shame, disown me, walk uponMy bleeding heart—but fly!
DIDIER.
Fly where? From whom?There's naught but you to fly from in this world;And I escape you, for the grave is deep.
THE JAILER.
The hour is passing.
MARION.
O my Didier, fly!
DIDIER.
I will not!
MARION.
Just for pity!
DIDIER.
Pity! why?
MARION.
To see you taken, bound! To see you—there!Only to think it makes me die of horror!Come! I will be a servant unto you.Come! Take me, when I have redeemed myself,Just to have something underneath your feet.The one you called "a wife" in times of trial—
DIDIER.
A wife! [Cannon sounds in the distance.This makes of you a widow, then!
MARION.
Didier!
THE JAILER.
The hour is past.
[Rolling of drums. Enter COUNCILOR OF THE GREAT CHAMBER, accompanied by penitents bearing torches, and by EXECUTIONER. A crowd of soldiers and people follow.
MARION.
Ah, Christ!

SCENE VII
The same. COUNCILOR, EXECUTIONER, Populace, Soldiers

COUNCILOR.
I'm ready,Gentlemen!
MARION (to DIDIER).
I told you that he'd come!
DIDIER (to COUNCILOR).
We're ready also.
COUNCILOR.
Which is named Gaspard,Marquis de Saverny?
[DIDIER points to SAVERNY, who is asleep.
[To EXECUTIONER.] Awaken him!
EXECUTIONER (shaking him).
How well he sleeps, my lord!
SAVERNY (rubbing his eyes).
Ah, how could youBreak in on such a pleasant sleep!
DIDIER.
'Tis onlyInterrupted, friend!

57

SAVERNY (*half awake: sees* MARION *and salutes her*).
Oh, I was dreamingAbout you, my beauty!
COUNCILOR.
Have you madeYour peace with God?
SAVERNY.
I have, sir.
COUNCILOR.
It is well.Please sign this paper!
SAVERNY (*takes the parchment, runs over it*).
'Tis the *procès-verbal.*Good! This is a most curious thing—accountOf my own death,
signed with my autograph!
[*Signs, and reads the paper again: to* COUNCILOR.
You have made three mistakes in spelling, sir.
[*Takes the pen and corrects them. To* EXECUTIONER.
You have awakened me; put me to sleep!
COUNCILOR (*to* DIDIER).
Didier!
[DIDIER *approaches:* COUNCILOR *gives pen to him.*
Your name is there.
MARION (*hiding her eyes*).
The grewsome thing!
DIDIER.
I could sign nothing with intenser joy!
[*The Guards form themselves into a line to lead them away.*
SAVERNY (*to some one in the crowd*).
Sir, step aside and let that young child see!
DIDIER (*to* SAVERNY).
My brother, 'tis for me you suffer death;Let us embrace each other! [*He
embraces* SAVERNY.
MARION (*running to him*).
And for meNo kisses, Didier!
DIDIER (*indicating* SAVERNY).
This is my friend, madame!
MARION (*clasping her hands*).
How hard you are upon me, a poor thing,Who always on my knees to king or
judgeHave begged mercy for you from every one!Pardon of them for you; pardon of you for
me!
DIDIER (*rushes to* MARION, *trembling, and bursting into tears*).
No, I cannot! The torture's horrible!No, I have loved too much to leave her so!It is
too hard to keep a cold, impassive faceWhen underneath the heart is breaking down.Come
to my arms, oh, woman, come!
[*Presses her convulsively to his heart.*
I love you!I'm about to die. Before them all,It is my loftiest joy to tell you this:I love
you!
MARION.
Didier!
DIDIER.
[*Embraces her again with rapture.*
To my heart, oh, come!You who behold this direful tragedy,I wonder if there's one of
you who wouldRefuse love unto one who'd given herselfEntirely and unceasingly to
him?Oh, I was wrong! Say, would you have me faceEternity without a pardon fromHer lips?
No! Stand by me and listen, love:Among all womankind—and those who hearWill prove me
right by their own hearts—the oneI love, the one in whom I trust, the oneI venerate is
you—is always you!For you were kind, devoted, loving, good.My life is almost ended. When
death's nearA clearer light illuminates all things.If you deceived me, 'twas excess of love;And
if you fell, have you not cruelly atoned?Perhaps your mother—life's so hard—forgotYou in

your cradle, as my mother did;When you were young and helpless, perhaps they soldYour innocence. Ah, lift up your white brow!And listen, all of you. At such an hourThe earth is a mere shadow and the heartSpeaks true. Well, at this moment, from the heightOf the dread scaffold—and there's naught so highWhen guiltless souls ascend it—here,I say to you, Marie, angel of light,Whose luster earth has dimmed, my love, my wife,In God's name, before whom I soon shall stand,I pardon you.

MARION (*suffocated with tears*).

Ah, Christ!

DIDIER.

It is your turn.Speak now, and pardon me!

[*He kneels before her.*

MARION.

Didier!

DIDIER.

Your pardon,Love! I was the most at fault, the mostUnkind. God has chastised you much through me.Weep for me when I'm gone, because to haveHurt you is such a burden to take henceInto eternity. Don't leave it on me;Pardon me!

MARION (*inaudibly*).

Have mercy on me—God!

DIDIER.

Just speak one word; put your sweet hands uponMy forehead. If your heart is full and youCan't speak, please make a sign. I'm dying; youMust comfort me.

[MARION *places her hand on his forehead; he rises, embraces her tenderly, with a smile of celestial joy.*

Farewell! Come, gentlemen!Let us move on!

MARION (*throws herself wildly between him and the Soldiers*).

Oh, no! Stop! This is madness!If you think you can behead him easily,You have forgotten I am here. Spare us!Oh, men! oh, soldiers, judge, people! Spare us!How do you want me to ask you? UponMy knees? Well, here I am! Now ifIn you there's anything that quivers atA woman's voice, if God has thrown no curseOn you—don't kill him![*To the spectators.*] Men and women—you!When you go back into your homes to-night,You'll find your mothers and your daughters; theyWill say to you, "It was a wicked crime.You might have saved him, and you did not. Shame!"Didier, they ought to know that I must followYou! They will not kill you if they wantTo keep me living!

DIDIER.

Let me die, Marie.'Tis better, dear one, for my wound is deep;It would have taken too much time to heal.Better for me to go; but if, some time—You see I'm weeping too—another comes,A happier man, more fortunate than I,Think of your old friend sleeping in the tomb.

MARION.

You shall not die! Are these men all inhuman?You must live!

DIDIER.

Don't ask things impossible.No; with your bright eyes, turn, illuminateMy grave for me. Embrace me. You will loveMe better, dead. I'll hold a sacred placeIn your dear memory. But if I lived,Lived near you with my lacerated soul—I, who have loved no one but you—you seeIt would be painful. I would make you weep.I'd have a thousand thoughts I could not speak.I'd seem to doubt you, watch you, worry you.You would be most unhappy. Let me die!

COUNCILOR (*to* MARION).

The Cardinal will pass by soon, madame!You can ask pardon for him then.

MARION.

Oh, yes!The Cardinal is coming—that is true.You'll see, then, gentlemen, that he will hear!My Didier, you shall hear me talk to him!The Cardinal! Indeed, you must be all insane,To think such an old man—a Christian too,The gracious Cardinal—will not be gladTo pardon you. Have you not pardoned me?

[*Nine o'clock strikes.* DIDIER *makes sign to all to hush.* MARION *listens with terror. After the nine strokes have sounded,* DIDIER *goes and stands close to* SAVERNY.

DIDIER (*to the spectators*).

You who have come to see the last of us,If any speak of us, bear witness all,That without faltering we have heard the hourBring us its summons to eternity.

[*The cannon sounds at the door of the tower; the black veil which concealed the opening in the wall, falls: the gigantic litter of* THE CARDINAL *appears, borne by twenty-four foot-guards, surrounded by twenty other guards bearing halberds and torches: the litter is scarlet and ornamented with the arms of the House of Richelieu. It crosses the back of the stage slowly. Great agitation among the crowd.*

MARION (*dragging herself up to the litter on her knees and wringing her hands*).

In your Christ's name! In name of all your race,Mercy for them, my lord!

A VOICE (*from the litter*).

No mercy!

[MARION *falls to the ground. The litter passes and the procession of the condemned men follows it. The crowd rush madly after them.*

MARION (*alone, lifts herself half way up, and drags herself along by her hands: looking around.*)

Ah!What did he say? Where are they gone? My love!My Didier! No one! Not a sound! Is itA dream—this place? the crowd?—or am I mad?

[*The people rush back in disorder. The litter reappears in the background on the side where it went off.* MARION *rises and gives a terrible cry.*

He's coming back!

GUARDS (*pushing the people aside*).

Make way!

MARION (*erect and half-wild, pointing to the litter*).

Look, all of you!It is the red man who goes by!

[*She falls senseless.*

Made in the USA
Las Vegas, NV
12 September 2021